Come Home to Little House
Five Generations of Pioneer Girls

WHERE LITTLE HOUSE BEGAN
Martha Morse
Laura's great-grandmother
born 1782

BOSTON'S LITTLE HOUSE GIRL
Charlotte Tucker
Laura's grandmother
born 1809

SPIRIT OF THE WESTERN FRONTIER
Caroline Quiner
Laura's mother
born 1839

AMERICA'S ORIGINAL PIONEER GIRL
Laura Ingalls
born 1867

PIONEER FOR A NEW CENTURY
Rose Wilder
Laura's daughter
born 1886

The Little House

MARTHA
(1782–1862)

Lewis Tucker

Lewis
(b. 1802)

Lydia
(b. 1805)

Thomas
(b. 1807)

CHARLOTTE
(1809–1884)

Joseph
(1834–1862)

Henry
(1835–1882)

Martha
(1837–1927)

Mary
(1865–1928)

LAURA
(1867–1957)

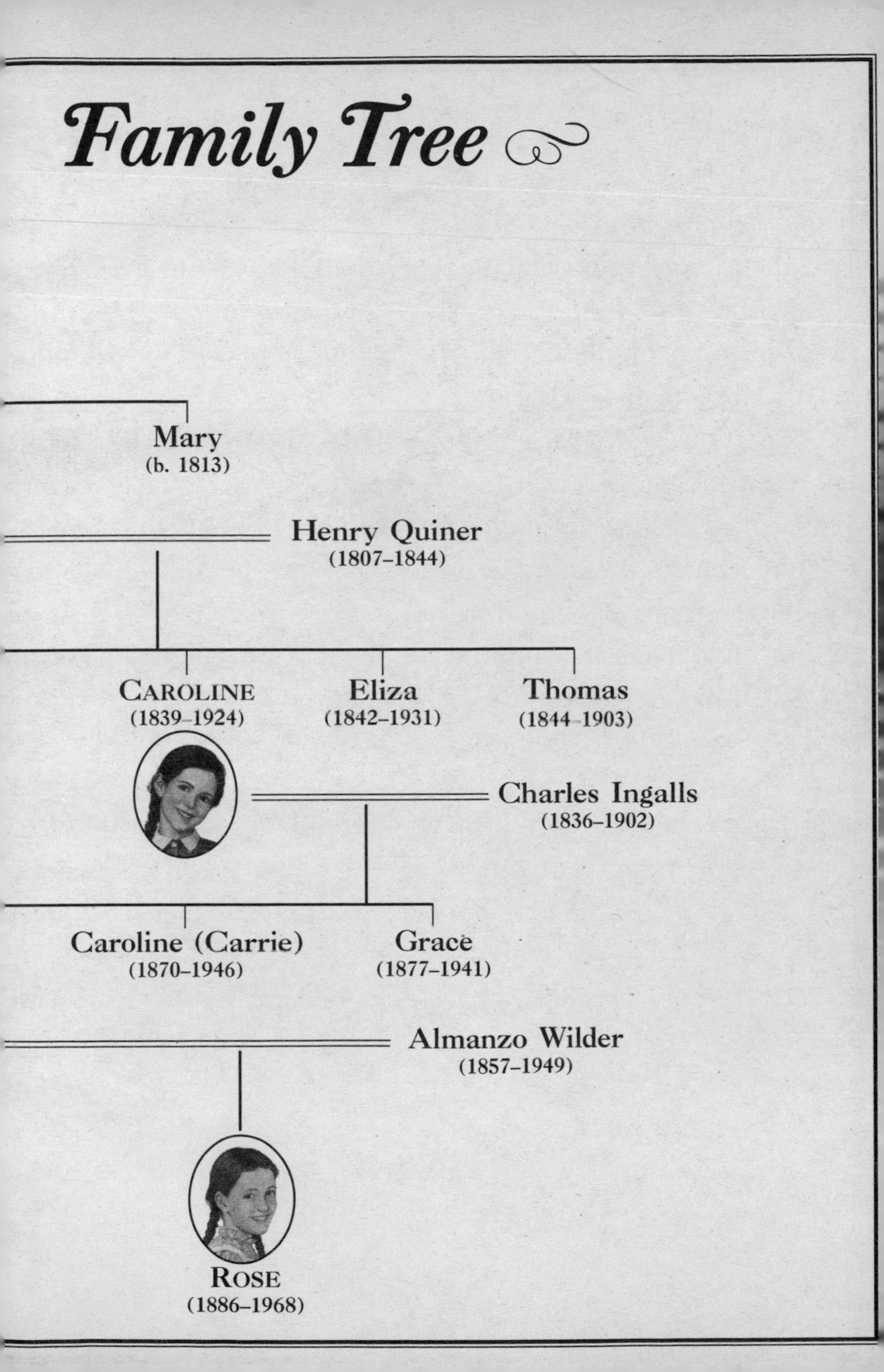
Family Tree
Mary
(b. 1813)
Henry Quiner
(1807–1844)
CAROLINE
(1839–1924)
Eliza
(1842–1931)
Thomas
(1844–1903)
Charles Ingalls
(1836–1902)
Caroline (Carrie)
(1870–1946)
Grace
(1877–1941)
Almanzo Wilder
(1857–1949)
ROSE
(1886–1968)

Beyond *the* Heather Hills

Melissa Wiley

Illustrations by Renée Graef

HarperTrophy®
An Imprint of HarperCollins*Publishers*

The author wishes to express heartfelt gratitude to Caroline Carr-Locke and Melissa Jaramillo for their assistance in researching the customs and culture of late eighteenth-century Scotland; and to my "panel of experts"—Deirdre Early, Jane McGuire, Joanna Oh, Susan Oh, and Bridget Rooney—for their insight and wisdom.

Printed in the United States of America. For information address HarperCollins Children's Books, a division of HarperCollins Publishers, 1350 Avenue of the Americas, New York, NY 10019.
www.littlehousebooks.com

Library of Congress Cataloging-in-Publication Data
Wiley, Melissa.
Beyond the heather hills / Melissa Wiley ; illustrations by Renée Graef.
p. cm.
Summary: Ten-year-old Martha Morse, who would grow up to become the great-grandmother of author Laura Ingalls Wilder, experiences the larger world outside of tiny Glencaraid, Scotland, when she goes to visit her married sister in Perth.
ISBN 0-06-027986-9 — ISBN 0-06-440715-2 (pbk.)
1. Morse, Martha—Juvenile fiction. [1. Morse, Martha—Fiction. 2. Wilder, Laura Ingalls, 1867–1957—Family—Fiction. 3. Sisters—Fiction. 4. Scotland—History—18th century—Fiction.] I. Graef, Renée, ill. II. Title.
PZ7.W64814 Be 2003 2002008336
[Fic]—dc21 CIP
AC

---

4 5 6 7 8 9 10
First Harper Trophy Edition, 2003

For the bonny Gunther girls:
Alice, Mary, Clair, and Bernadette;
and for their mother,
Alice the Best

Contents

Beyond *the* Heather Hills

The Edge of New

The carriage had two windows, and Martha could not decide which one had the better view. She was in new country now, a place she had never seen before. All her life she had wanted to know what lay beyond the moor east of her father's land, beyond Glencaraid and the Creag and Auld Mary's quiet hut. Now she was here. *Beyond* stretched out on either side of her: rippling hillsides thick with heather and broom, threaded here and there with faint paths that might have been made by cattle or shepherds or the fairy folk, for all Martha could tell.

She wished Father would let her sit up top beside Sim, the curly-haired driver, but of course that was so far out of the question, there was no use in asking. It was enough that he had brought her on this trip. Mum had been hesitant to let her go. Such a journey, over rough roads, for a ten-year-old lass without mother or governess to watch over her—Mum had had her doubts over the wisdom of the notion. Perth lay a great many miles east of Glencaraid.

But Grisie's letters pleaded for a visit. It was six months since she had married Kenneth MacDougal and moved away from the valley. Grisie loved her new husband and her fine house in the city; but she was homesick. Father had declared that since Grisie could not come to Glencaraid, Glencaraid should come to Grisie. Mum could not leave the Stone House at this time of year, with the wagonloads of milk and butter coming down each week from the cattle's summer pasturing grounds in the mountain glens. She must be on hand to oversee the weighing and to keep the accounts. And so—

"Martha shall go," Father had said. "I'll take her myself when I go to Perth to do the trading, and she shall come home wi' the lads in the school holidays."

Mum had agreed at last, reluctantly.

"Though I dinna ken how we'll do without you," she had said, squeezing Martha close. "My last bairn, grown so big."

Martha had felt at once jubilant and alarmed—which was quite an uncomfortable way to feel. She had never been so far from home before; she had never been away from Mum for longer than a few days. Now she was to spend more than a month far from the Stone House. She would miss the wool-waulking, the cheesemaking, the games on St. Columba's day. But she would at long last see Perth—the Fair City, it was called. She would see Grisie, and Kenneth, and Mr. John Smeaton's famous bridge over the Tay. She would see things with her own eyes that some people lived their whole lives only hearing about.

Miss Crow, Martha's governess, was given

a long holiday, which she planned to spend with some cousins near Loch Katrine. But first she had helped Mum make three new dresses for Martha, for a laird's daughter must not be seen in town in patched or faded frocks, with her knees showing under a hem that had been let down as far as a hem could be let. The blue-and-yellow-striped linen frock, the sheer white muslin, and the shimmering golden silk were folded carefully in Martha's trunk, beneath her light woolen shawl (blue plaid), her new bonnet (straw, with a sky-blue ribbon), and her new linen collar (lace trimmed, with cherries embroidered upon it). Martha had never had so many new clothes all at once. She heartily wished she could give some of them away, particularly the silk, which had a row of buttons up its back so long that Martha feared she would miss breakfast every time she had to wear it.

Still, an excess of buttons was a small price to pay for a journey such as this. She was going to Perth! Her brothers had been attending school there for years; now, at last, Martha was to see it for herself.

The carriage rattled past a flock of sheep, their coats shorn close for the summer. The shepherd, a tall, lean boy in dingy breeches, stood leaning on his staff, watching the carriage go by. Martha stared back through the small square window, wondering who he was. It was strange to see a stranger. She knew every soul on her father's estate and in the village across Loch Caraid. This boy was someone unknown. The shepherd caught Martha's eye and respectfully lifted his battered felt hat, his face impassive and wind reddened. She waved at him without thinking, just as the carriage was leaving him behind, and in her last bumpy glimpse of him, she saw how he broke into a grin and waved back. Then Martha jumped and drew back against the carriage seat. She stole a glance at Father to see if he was watching.

He was, with reproving eyes. Martha felt the color coming to her cheeks, and her hand went out to straighten her skirts. She did not want Father to think she was being childish.

He was the one who had insisted that Martha was old enough to make such a journey when Mum had had doubts. This was utterly unlike the usual way of things. Father was much more apt to say Mum gave Martha too much liberty; Martha must learn to behave in accordance with her station in life. She was a laird's daughter and must comport herself like one. She was ten years old now, a wee 'un no longer. Great girls of ten must not wave at strange shepherds in passing fields.

To break the uncomfortable silence, she said, "Whose land is this, Father?"

Father looked out the window. "This whole region, from Lochearnhead to Crieff, was once the holdings o' the Drummond clan—your mother's people. The chief kept a castle at Crieff. 'Twas said he could muster a thousand men at the blowing o' a horn. But that was long ago."

"I wish I might have seen it," said Martha wistfully. Staring across the moor, she could almost see the crowds of men standing upon the heather, in their kilted plaids and tasseled stockings. The rough wind that beat against the carriage seemed to hold an echo of pipes shrilling above the ranks.

Father smiled. "Ye'd have liked it little, lassie, if I'd been called to battle, happen to die on a rival's sword."

"Like Mum's father," said Martha. The thought of it made a chill crinkle up her spine. To think of Father lying dead upon the heather, with the wild outcry of battle swirling on above his bleeding corpse . . .

The carriage jolted and swayed along the bumpy path. Cloud shadows grazed slowly over the grass, like great gray cattle. To the north, the distant mountains; to the south, the undulating moor. They passed a small croft, its fields sown in barley, rye, and turnips. A shabby cottage sat forlornly beside a plot of kale. Smoke rose from the hole in the center of its thatched roof, and a goat stood in the open doorway, greens hanging from its chewing mouth. Its yellow eyes glared at Martha. She watched a barefoot girl trailing a cow between two rows of barley, her hair hanging loose down her back. The girl wore a faded gray plaid in loose folds and fastened with a large pin. She, too, like the goat and the shepherd lad, stopped to watch the carriage go by. The cow, as if sensing her distraction, veered into the ripening grain, and the girl slapped its bony rump with the flat of her hand, steering it back between the rows.

The carriage rolled on. It was strange, Martha thought, to pass people and know that you would probably never see them again. She wondered what the girl's name was, and how old she was. She wondered if the girl was wondering the same thing about her.

A Laird's Daughter

They stopped at Crieff that night. Father helped Martha out of the carriage and told her she might walk about a little, so long as she did not wander far.

"I'll go look out the innkeeper," he murmured, nodding toward a building that stood close to the road. He called instructions to Sim, the driver, and disappeared into the inn.

Martha's legs were glad of the chance to stretch after the long, jolting, tooth-rattling hours in the carriage. She stood in the road, turning a slow circle, taking it all in. There was the inn, a large stone house built half into a hillside. She had never slept in an inn before. Her heart was soaring. She had always longed to see this place. Crieff was a fair-sized town, a great deal larger than the tiny village of Clachan near Father's estate. Father's steward, Sandy, often came here to trade Mum's fine linen thread for tea, sugar, and spices. To the north, a steep hill rose broodingly above the town, like a sentinel standing guard.

Sim jumped down from the wagon seat to tend to the horses. He saw Martha looking at the hill.

"That be the Knock," he said, pointing with his thumb. "The views from up yonder will fair take yer breath away."

The horses nosed the grass alongside the road. Martha went to pet them, stroking the dusty neck of the chestnut mare. The mare rolled her eyes sideways and shook her head without raising it, as if to say, *Sorry, no time to chat; I'm that hungry I could eat a meadow!*

Sim chuckled.

"Unsociable creature, isna she?" he said.

"Ah, but I ken how she feels. I could do wi' a bite to eat meself." He patted his stomach, looking expectantly toward the inn.

"Och, aye," Martha agreed. But she did not want to go into the inn quite yet. Her eyes were hungrier than her stomach was; she wanted to stay out and look at the town.

Father had told her that in years past, Crieff had been the site of the greatest cattle fair in all the Highlands. It was easy to imagine a crowd of cattle bawling in the square, denting the ground with their hooves. The fair had moved to Falkirk in the south long before Martha was born, and she was sorry. She would have liked to see it: the streets packed with jostling steers as far as the eye could see, the air crazed with shouts and lowing.

But even without the cattle fair, there was more than enough to see and hear. A sharp, monotonous clanging issued from a building down the way; Martha followed the sound and saw that it was a blacksmith's shop. The smith, a red-bearded, thick-armed giant of a man, was beating a glowing rod with a hammer. Martha stood outside the smithy, watching him. She loved the stinging smell of hot iron. Sometimes the village smith came across the lake to Glencaraid, to set up a makeshift forge in one of Father's outbuildings. Miss Crow would let Martha go and watch with the farmers' children, so long as Martha had finished her lessons. Miss Crow said ironwork was an ancient and noble art.

The blacksmith threw down his hammer and plunged the pounded iron into a bucket of water, sending a cloud of steam hissing into the air. He glanced at Martha, standing in his doorway, but took no notice of her. She felt a jolt of surprise. No one in Glencaraid would neglect to greet her. But of course he could not know that she was the laird's daughter—and then it struck her that she was not *the* laird's daughter—she was *a* laird's daughter, one of many, surely, to visit this town. Crieff was not part of her father's holdings. For almost the first time in her life, she was standing upon soil that did not belong to her family.

This was an uncomfortable thought. With

it came a disagreeable, dawning consciousness that she was perhaps not quite as important a person as she was accustomed to thinking. She had not known until now that she thought of herself as important at all, simply because her father owned the land on which the people around her lived. This second glimmer of new understanding was more disagreeable still. She had always felt disgusted by people who gave themselves airs. Suppose she had been guilty of the same thing, all this time? It was an idea not to be borne—she brushed it away.

She looked around for something else to see, to distract herself. A man was coming down the road toward her, carrying something heavy slung over his shoulder. She was so determined not to expect special acknowledgment that when the man drew up in surprise and doffed his cap to her, she was startled.

"Miss Martha, as I live and breathe!" the man uttered. "Sure and ye're a muckle way from home."

"I—I'm going to Perth with Father," she

stammered, trying to place the man. He seemed familiar; she had seen him before, somewhere.

"Aye, o' course," said the man, scratching beneath the band of his cap with a very dirty thumb. "Didna me bairns fair talk me deaf aboot it?"

Martha recognized him then. He was one of Father's tenants, a man named Gow. Martha knew his family well. His wife had nearly died of a terrible cough the year before—*would* have died, Auld Mary said, if Martha and Miss Crow hadn't discovered her in time. Auld Mary had nursed her back to health, and Martha had visited often. The Gow children, Sorcha and Ranald, had become special friends of Martha's, though they were much younger. They often made the long trek from their cottage at the farthest reach of Father's land to visit Martha in the Stone House, bringing her bunches of flowers or baskets of bilberries. She had scarcely ever seen their father, though. He spent little time at home.

"Is yer father aboot, then?" Mr. Gow asked

her, a trifle nervously. He stood up a little straighter, trying to make light of the bundle on his back, as if it were no heavier than a sack of goose feathers.

"Aye," said Martha carelessly, "he's at the inn. We're stopping the night."

"Are ye? Well, now. That's fine." He swiped at his forehead with the back of a hand, leaving a smudge of dirt and perspiration. "I hear 'tis a good clean inn, where they change the beddin' twice a month whether it needs it or no. And a fine ale, too."

He took a few steps backward as he spoke, and ducking his head to Martha, he mumbled to her to pay his respects to her father. He struck off down a side lane behind the smithy, walking rapidly away. Martha stared after him, watching how the heavy bundle on his back bowed him down.

Doune House

Father frowned when Martha told him of her curious encounter with Mr. Gow.

"Gow's a man o' weak will," said Father. "He ought to be mindin' his barley field instead o' traipsin' aboot the county, the fool. Were it no for his family, I'd turn him off the land."

"What do you think he had in that sack, Father?" Martha asked, but Father only shrugged.

"A brace o' pheasant, I doubt not, that he

poached off another man's land. He'd no want me to catch him at that."

The inn's mistress had shown them to a large parlor, dark and chilly, with a long table in the center and a dozen or so unmatched chairs against the walls. There were a couple of dozing cats, a halfhearted fire, and a smeary window that looked out upon the kitchen garden. The mistress brought them a meal of mutton and barley cakes. The bread was chewy and tasteless; Cook would have scorned it. Father threw his down upon his plate, half eaten, with a gesture of disgust.

"We might as well eat stones," he murmured. "At least the meat is tender."

It was tender, but no less bland than the bread, as if it had been stewed without salt. Martha had imagined public houses to be much more pleasant places than this cold, dingy inn. Never had she slept in such a lumpy and dirty bed as she did that night. She slept in her clothes, as Mum had told her to, and the buttons pressed into her back wherever the bed lumps did not.

She was not used to sleeping alone. At home, she shared a bed with Miss Crow. She told herself she was being silly, but she could not help feeling a little afraid. The dark room was full of strange rustlings: rats, probably. She pulled the coarse sheets up tight beneath her chin and stared anxiously into the darkness, afraid at every heartbeat that a rat would run across the bed. She wished Mum were there. Thinking of Mum made her eyes sting. She wished Father had not taken a separate room—she wished she had never left Glencaraid—and most especially she wished Grisie had stayed at home where she belonged. Martha clutched the sheets and lay there silently fuming at her sister. It was almost a relief to have something to be angry about; it made her forget about missing home, and about the rats.

She slept poorly, starting awake at each tiny creak of the house. It was the sort of house that had a great many creaks. In the morning she sprang gladly out of bed, throwing back the bedcovers so she would not see the top of them. She didn't know what she expected to see—rats would hardly leave pawprints on the coverlet—but all the same, she did not want to look at it.

She washed her face in tepid water at a basin on the table beside the bed and hurried into her shoes. Father met her in the parlor.

"Father!" she cried, running to throw her arms about him.

He looked down at her half smiling, half puzzled, and patted her head awkwardly.

"Er—good morning, lass. How'd ye pass the night?"

"Och, Father, it was dreadful, it was!"

She began to tell him about the rats and the bed lumps, but he silenced her with a swift shake of his head. He gave a little nod with his chin toward the doorway that led to the inn's kitchen.

"Hush," he murmured in her ear. "Would you have the servants hear you?"

Martha bit her lip. How often had Mum

told her a child must never complain? Especially in front of servants. *It's a good tongue that says no ill, and a better heart that thinks none,* Mum would say.

Martha nodded to show Father she understood, but really she did not understand it at all. It seemed to her it would be a good thing for the innkeeper to know what was wrong with his rooms. How was he to improve them if no one complained?

Father motioned her to be seated at the same table at which they had eaten the night before. A sullen-faced serving girl brought a jug of whey and a platter of the same bland barley cakes, now more stale than chewy. The whey was very good, however, rich and cool. The innkeeper's wife must have made cheese recently, Martha guessed, to have such fresh whey, which was the liquid left over after milk had been curdled into cheese. She drank it hungrily, wishing there had been more in the jug.

That day's ride was not so interesting as

yesterday's had been. Martha was stiff and sore, tired of the constant bumping. She wished they had left the carriage behind and simply ridden the horses. She wished Perth were not so far away.

"How much farther?" she asked her father.

"We'll be there this afternoon, barring trouble," he answered. Martha leaned sleepily against the side of the carriage and watched the square of earth and sky jolt past.

Gradually the scenery changed. The bare sweeping moor gave way to wooded hills, with a croft in every hollow. Here and there Martha glimpsed a fine house upon a hill, or an avenue of trees that hinted at a house just beyond. The road was better here, more firmly packed. It was a road that knew it was a road, not a mere track that sometimes played at being one. The occasional villages began to be closer together.

There was something different to see on either side of the carriage—an old stone church, a field blanketed with sun-bleached

linen—but Martha did not look back and forth between the two windows as she had done. She leaned back against the cushioned seat and let the view rush past her like a river. Her eyelids grew heavy, and the drifting trees blurred together.

She thought she was back at the inn, in the lumpy bed, where great black rats were making bold dashes across her bed. She called out for Father, but he was far away and could not hear her. He was back home in Glencaraid. Martha could see him, and Mum, but she could not get to them because of the rats. Then Mr. Gow came along with his sack and began popping the rats into it, one by one.

Martha's teeth rattled, hard, and she was jolted awake. Her tongue was stinging; she had bitten it in her sleep. She shook her head, dispelling the unsettling dream, and turned in a rush to tell Father all about it. But Father was leaning out of the carriage talking to Sim.

One of the wheel spokes had snapped in two. Sim set about replacing it. He kept a supply of extra spokes beneath his seat.

Father and Martha climbed out of the carriage to stretch their legs while Sim worked. Martha was surprised to learn that they had reached the outskirts of Perth. She looked around, taking it in: the houses built close together, the cobbled streets, the signboards hanging from little wooden arms that jutted out over the doors of shops. She felt full of questions and wished Mum were there, or Miss Crow. They could always be counted on to answer questions with enthusiasm. With Father, it was more chancy. Sometimes he was in the mood to talk, and sometimes he wasn't. He had been quiet in the carriage all day. Martha felt hesitant to try him out. She had never before spent this much time alone with Father. She wanted him to be as excited about the journey as she was, but of course he had made this trip many times before. It was not new to him, and the broken wheel spoke had made him cross.

"There we are, noo," said Sim at last, slapping the rim of the wheel with the flat of his hand. "We'll get along well enough. Shall I help ye back in, miss?"

The last bit of the journey was almost too short. There was so much to see. The narrow streets rang with noise. Hooves clattered, cartwheels rumbled, boys shouted. A man stood on a corner with a wooden tray held up by a strap around his neck; he was selling something, but Martha had only a tantalizing glimpse of mussels before the carriage left him behind. Dogs ran alongside the carriage, barking. The air smelled of fish and smoke and other things besides, not all of them nice. There were piles of refuse in the streets, and beside each front door was a heap of rubbish. More dogs were scrounging in the rubbish heaps for potato peelings, and sometimes Martha saw little grubby children digging through the heaps as well. That made her shudder, for the heaps smelled as if chamber pots had been emptied into them as well as kitchen scrap pails.

"Ah, here's the Watergate Street," said

Father, pleased. He leaned out the window to call instructions to Sim. To Martha, he said, "We'll be in your sister's parlor five minutes hence."

Martha's heart leaped. How she had missed Grisie!

The carriage slowed to a stop before a house in the middle of a long row of close-packed houses. Like all the others, it had no dooryard. Its stone walls rose straight up from below street level in three neat stories. DOUNE HOUSE, read letters carved above the door.

Sim rapped on the door, while Father and Martha waited in the carriage. Martha peered eagerly out of the window, half expecting Grisie herself to open the door. But it was opened by a thin, middle-aged maidservant in a plain, dark dress. Her gray hair was parted on her forehead in two grizzled wings, the rest of it hidden beneath a linen cap. She looked at Sim in a rather glaring way.

"The laird of Glencaraid and his daughter, Miss Martha," said Sim in a voice much deeper than his usual tones. The maidservant peered past him to the carriage just beyond and nodded sharply.

"Mrs. MacDougal is expecting ye." She added, almost accusingly, "Ye've arrived on the butler's half day. I'll show ye in."

Sim turned to help Martha out of the carriage.

"Merry auld soul, isna she?" he muttered under his breath. Martha nearly laughed out loud. Father stepped down behind her and, taking her arm, accompanied her to the door. Sim stayed behind to untie the baggage from the roof of the carriage.

The pinched-lipped maidservant ducked in a curtsey so slight as to be almost nonexistent, then stepped to the side and gestured for Father and Martha to enter. Martha felt a wave of indignation at the oddly cold reception. But it was forgotten, next minute, as she looked in awe at the inside of the house in which her sister now lived.

She stood in a large entry hall, painted a

delicate green. The floor was made of neat gray stone slabs. A pair of mahogany chairs stood against one wall, and a gleaming semicircular table stood opposite, beneath a large portrait of man in a black coat and white neckerchief. Beyond an open door was a glimpse of a passage and a wooden staircase.

The maidservant led them through the door and down the passage, stopping outside another open door.

"Mr. Morse o' Glencaraid, madam," she croaked, dropping another negligible curtsey.

Martha heard Grisie's voice, soft and dignified. "Thank you, Kitty. That will be all."

The maidservant stepped out of the doorway, allowing Father and Martha to enter the room. She left, closing the door behind them.

There was Grisie, standing near a window. She seemed older, nearly as old as Miss Crow. Her hair was heaped high upon her head. Martha felt oddly shy, seeing her sister so grown-up and dignified. When Grisie saw Father, her hand went automatically to the nape of her neck as if to pull the knot of curls lower, and then she colored a little and let her hand fall. Martha grinned. Grisie was a married woman now, and Father could not furrow his brow and say that girls of her age ought not to put up their hair.

Grisie's face was alight, and she came swiftly toward the door to kiss Father. She threw her arms around Martha and squeezed her tight.

"Dearest!"

That made Martha laugh. Grisie had never once called her "dearest" in her life. She hugged her sister back, hard.

"I'm that glad to see you, Grisie," she murmured. "I do wish you didna live so far from home."

"This is my home now," said Grisie. She held Martha at arm's length and looked her over. "Mercy, how you've grown. You're almost ready for long skirts!"

"She's but a child yet, Mrs. MacDougal," said Father lightly, slipping an arm round Martha's shoulder. They were all laughing now, because it was so strange to hear Grisie addressed by her new name. Martha would have hated to be called a child by Grisie, but she did not mind when Father said it. She did not want to be a grown-up yet, and have to fuss over clothes, and curl her hair with a hot iron rod, and be called "Mrs." She could not think of Grisie as "Mrs. MacDougal"—it was quite impossible. Martha could not think of her sister as mistress of a house, any more than she would think herself a murderous queen simply because she had taken the part of Lady MacBeth in reading a play with Miss Crow.

"A fine room, this," said Father, nodding approvingly. It was a large parlor, painted the same pale green as the hall. A white chimneypiece carved with vines ornamented the fireplace, with a narrow mantel upon which stood four or five dainty china vases. Over the mantel was another portrait, this one of a woman with the long, trailing skirt of her white gown caught up gracefully in one outstretched hand. She had a melancholy face and a lot of coiled hair.

In the center of the room, a large square table stood beneath a sparkling crystal chandelier. Six candles stood up from little crystal candleholders around a wide central stem. Dozens of delicate tear-shaped prisms dangled down. It hung high above the table, out of reach, and made Martha wonder how anyone ever managed to light the candles.

"My husband bade me express his regret at not being here to greet you," said Grisie. Martha could not stifle a snort. *My husband*, indeed!

Grisie ignored her, explaining, "He was called away on an errand for my father-in-law. We expect him home within the week. I do hope he returns before you leave, Father."

"Is Balliecruin in town now?" Father asked. He meant Kenneth's father, the elder Mr. MacDougal. He was laird of a very large estate called Balliecruin, north of Father's land. The proper way for Father to address him was by the name of his estate, just as other folk called Father "Glencaraid."

Grisie nodded.

"Aye. He has been with us these last six weeks. I expect he'll stay another month at least."

Father nodded, pleased. "Splendid. I shall be glad to see him."

"Indeed," said Grisie—rather unconvincingly, Martha thought. "He had an engagement this afternoon, but I should think he'll be home in time for tea. I suppose you must be famished!"

"Aye!" cried Martha. Father laughed and said they had better wash up first. Grisie picked up a little bell from the table and rang it. A few minutes later, a uniformed, white-wigged servant appeared, bowing low.

"Show Mr. Morse to his room, John," said Grisie. "And send Kitty to Miss Martha."

"Aye, madam."

Father followed the servant out of the room. Grisie turned to Martha, her eyes sparkling.

"Och, it's lovely to have you here!" she cried. She sat down on a cushioned chair near the hearth and motioned for Martha to take the chair beside her. She was eager for all the news from home—"While we're waiting for Kitty," she said.

Eagerly, Martha began to tell her all about the new kitchenmaid and the new housemaid, for Mollie too had married and left the Stone House.

"And Nannie has a new bairn!" she enthused; but Grisie seemed uninterested in the news of present and former servants. She wanted news of the cousins at Fairlie, across the loch, and a precise description of Mum's new summer gowns.

"Did she make the sleeves exactly as I wrote her?" she pressed. "They're being worn elbow length now. We were always so terribly out o' fashion in Glencaraid."

"Mum makes any gown look beautiful," said Martha indignantly.

"Och, aye, I ken," soothed Grisie, "but she might at least try to keep up with times. Look here, she's given you just the one ruffle at the hem. Mrs. Reid's daughters have three rows o' ruffles on their new summer frocks."

"I'd rather have no ruffles at all," said Martha, who disliked frills.

Grisie laughed merrily.

"Och, you dear lass! How I've missed you! I confess I've been a bit lonely, with my husband away."

Martha suppressed a grin. There it was again, the careless "my husband."

"Where has he gone?" she asked. She liked her brother-in-law very much. She had looked forward to seeing him almost as much as to seeing Grisie.

Grisie sighed.

"To Balliecruin. Och, Martha!" She leaned forward, speaking in a whisper. "You've no idea how dreadful it is, having my father-in-law about. Mrs. MacDougal does not like the city and keeps to their house at Balliecruin. But Mr. MacDougal comes to Perth quite often, and he stays here, o' course. This is his house, you know. He is terribly particular about how things are done. I dare not so much as move a cushion. If I do, he's sure to notice."

Martha grimaced, and Grisie added in an alarmed afterthought, "You must take great care to mind your manners, and not go making messes!"

Martha began to retort that she wasn't a baby anymore, but Grisie went on talking.

"And you're not to sit about talking with the servants, as you're used to doing at home. The auld man willna stand for it. Since Kenneth went away, I hardly speak to another soul from dawn to dusk. Excepting callers, o' course."

"He sounds terrible cross, Mr. MacDougal," said Martha, frowning. She remembered Kenneth's father, a handsome, sober old man. He had seemed courteous and mild the few times Martha had met him. She had heard tales, however, of his harsh treatment of his tenants and servants.

"Is it true," she asked Grisie, also whispering, "that he turned John Dunbie's widow and children out of their house after John drowned in Loch Tay?"

"Hush," said Grisie quickly. "We mustn't

gossip. Look, here's Kitty."

The grim-faced maidservant entered the parlor and looked inquiringly at Grisie.

"Ah, there you are, Kitty. You may show Miss Martha to her room now," said Grisie, sounding exactly like Mum. Martha wished Kitty had taken longer. There were so many things she wanted to talk to Grisie about; they had only just been getting started.

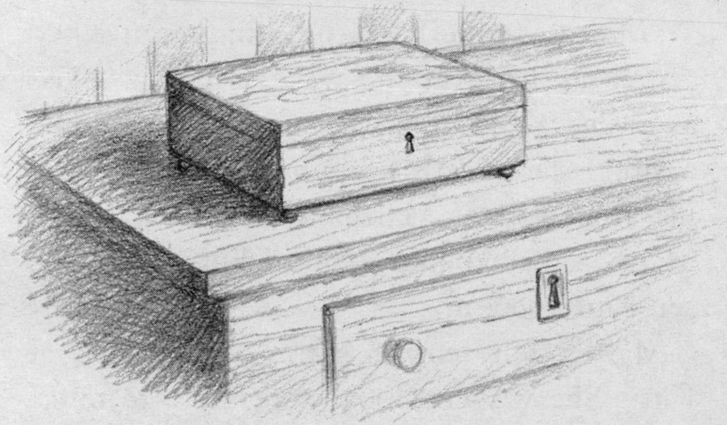

Dead Cora

Kitty led the way in silence to Martha's room. It was a small, elegant chamber on the second floor, its walls papered a creamy pale yellow with stripes of a slightly darker shade. Ivory curtains embroidered with red fringe enclosed a mahogany four-poster bed. There was a chest of drawers against the opposite wall, and two pretty chintz-covered chairs stood in the center of the room.

"This was Miss Cora's chamber," said the scowling Kitty. "Her that died so sudden."

"Miss Cora?" said Martha, confused.

"Master Kenneth's sister," muttered Kitty. "Apple o' his eye, she was. As bonny a lass as ivver walked upon the earth. *She* sang like a lark," she added, her stone-gray eyes glaring accusingly at Martha, as if to imply that Martha croaked like a raven but lacked the sense to know it.

Martha felt herself glaring right back at Kitty. She wished Cook were there to retort that Martha too had a voice like a bird. It was not the sort of thing she could say about her own self.

But she was sorely tempted to.

Kitty went to the chest and opened the top drawer. Martha saw that her clothes had already been unpacked and laid neatly in the drawer.

"This drawer is yers, miss," said Kitty. "The others is locked. Miss Cora's things be still inside, God rest her sweet soul."

Martha bristled inwardly. Kitty need not make such a point of saying the drawers were locked, as if Martha might be tempted to meddle with someone else's things. But Kitty was not finished. She touched a small wooden box on top of the chest of drawers.

"This was Miss Cora's workbox," she intoned. "It's just as she left it, the day she died, poor lass." She added, as Martha had known she would: "'Tis locked."

Everything Martha could think of to say in reply was impertinent, so she pressed her mouth shut.

Kitty seemed to have run out of locked drawers then, for she turned abruptly and left the room. Martha felt half afraid to touch anything, lest she smudge it or break it, which would surely confirm the bad opinion the servant seemed to have of her. She would ask Grisie, next chance she got, why Kitty disliked her so. Perhaps Kitty was the sort of person who did not like anyone—except of course for poor dead Cora.

Martha had not known that Kenneth had a sister who died. She wondered how long ago it had happened, and how old the girl had been. There was something unsettling about staying in a room that had belonged to a dead girl. Suppose she had died in this very bed?

Her gaze fell upon a small object on a little table beside the bed: a silver oval containing a miniature painting. It was a portrait of a young girl.

"You must be Cora," Martha murmured.

The girl in the picture could not have been much older than Martha herself. She had a high, pale forehead and dark, wispy hair. Her round eyes had a startled, unhappy look, as if she had just sat on a hedgehog. Martha wondered if she had looked like that all the time. She would have had to sit still for a very long time for the painting. Yet surely the painter had not captured Cora's appearance exactly, for Kitty had said she was a bonny lass. The girl in this picture was most certainly not bonny. She looked peevish and rather dim. Martha thought it was cruel of the painter, leaving behind such an unflattering image. Now the real girl was gone and could not prove the painter wrong.

Another servant entered the room, carrying a basin of water for the washstand. This one was a young girl, perhaps a few years older than Martha. Martha smiled at her, hoping she would be friendlier than Kitty. But the girl only curtseyed without meeting Martha's eye, and hurried out of the room without speaking. It made Martha feel very queer inside, and rather lonely. She understood already how Grisie felt in this strange house, so unlike her own cozy home.

"I wish Mum were here," she said to Cora's picture. "Or Miss Crow."

Cora stared at Martha with aggrieved eyes. *What are you doing in my room?* she seemed to be saying.

Martha picked up the picture.

"Dinna worry," she said, sighing. "I'll not lay a finger on your things. Couldna if I wanted to. There's a keyhole every blessed place I look. I wonder they didna put a lock on the bedcurtains."

She could almost hear Kitty croaking, "She's still in the bed, poor lass, same as the day she died."

The thought made Martha shudder. She set Cora's picture back in its place on the table, wishing, a little bit—though she was ashamed of the thought and pushed it down inside her—that she had never left Glencaraid.

The Laird of Balliecruin

The older Mr. MacDougal arrived at Doune House just as tea was being served. Martha noticed that Kitty was as grim faced and stony eyed in her master's presence as out of it; that made her feel better. Perhaps it was simply her way. Perhaps she would improve on further acquaintance. Even Cook could seem cross and formidable to those who did not know her well.

Old Balliecruin, Mr. MacDougal, was a tall, dignified-looking gentleman. He wore a white wig with small neat curls on the sides, tied in a short tail in the back. He wore black breeches, tight black stockings, and a long-tailed black coat over a striped silk waistcoat.

He greeted Father warmly, clapping him on the shoulder, and returned Martha's curtsey with a solemn, cordial bow.

"Ye're growing tall, girl," he remarked. "Methinks ye'll outstrip your sister."

"I think Grisie will always be taller, sir; she wears such high slippers," said Martha, uttering the first thing that came into her head. Grisie shot her a poisonous glance. Martha ducked a little, realizing she had embarrassed her sister but uncertain how.

"Aye, my daughter-in-law is fond of frippery," said Mr. MacDougal. Grisie's cheeks flamed red. Father was absorbed in studying a painting on the parlor wall, paying no attention to the conversation around him, as he was wont to do.

"Very fine landscape, this," he said to Mr. MacDougal. "Does the place lie near here?"

Mr. MacDougal went to stand beside him, and they launched into an animated discussion of the country north of Perth. Martha slipped over to Grisie's side and squeezed her hand. Grisie said nothing, but after a few seconds she squeezed back.

Those were the only words Mr. MacDougal spoke to Martha the whole evening. After the first greeting, he seemed to take no more notice of her than he would of an empty chair. Martha and Grisie took their tea in silence, while Father and Mr. MacDougal talked. There was cake, plum preserves, and cold sliced chicken. Martha ate three pieces of shortbread, rich and buttery sweet. She reached for a fourth, expecting someone to stop her; but Grisie seemed caught in a reverie, and the men were deep in discussion. Mum was not here to scold in her merry way, nor Miss Crow to comment with a lift of her eyebrow. Martha sat back, her hand falling to her lap, feeling suddenly too homesick for shortbread.

After tea, Mr. MacDougal took Father to his sitting room for a glass of brandy. Kitty came in to clear the tea things in thin-lipped silence.

"Come, Martha, you have not yet seen my sitting room," said Grisie, catching her by the hand. They went up the stairs and down the same passage from which Dead Cora's room opened. Grisie's room was three doors past Martha's.

"Isn't he fearful?" Grisie asked, dropping into a chintz-covered chair. "How he barks!"

Martha shrugged. "Cook's a good deal more fearsome when a cross mood comes upon her!"

"Nay, it isna the same thing at all. Cook's that fond o' you, she'd face a dragon to save you, no matter how cross you might have made her. I dinna think my father-in-law thinks anything o' me, unless it's that I'm a frivolous goose in high heels."

Martha winced. "I didna mean—"

"I ken you didna," Grisie interrupted. "Never mind."

She turned to her looking glass and raised a hand to smooth one of the shining curls upon her neck. Martha stared at her admiringly. Her sister was lovely. But how long it must take to dress her hair!

"Grisie," she said, "tell me about Kenneth's sister. When did she die?"

"Och, Cora!" said Grisie. "The poor lass."

She told Martha how Cora, Kenneth's only sister, had been a fine, hearty girl of thirteen when she died.

"A dish of tainted fish, it was. The whole household took ill. Cora died, and one of the servants. Mrs. MacDougal nearly died when she lost Cora. Kenneth was eighteen at the time. Cora would be a young lady now, if she'd lived. Ken says she was as merry as a skylark on a June morning. It's a terrible sad tale."

"I saw her picture," Martha said. "I didna think she looked so very merry."

"Och, that," said Grisie. "Mrs. MacDougal painted it. She canna bear to look at it, it's such a poor likeness; and yet she canna bring herself to part wi' it, for it's the only portrait Cora ever sat for. My mother-in-law says she will never forgive herself for failing to hire a portrait taker to paint Cora's picture."

"How awful," said Martha. She felt very sorry for Cora.

That evening, when she returned to her room, she picked up the picture once more and studied it in a determined effort to see the bonny, merry girl Cora had been really. The wide-open eyes continued to stare with a dull, irritated expression, as if the girl had no thoughts in her head except unpleasant ones. But perhaps if they had not been quite so wide open, and if the mouth had been smiling instead of bored, and the hair had been worn loose upon the shoulders instead of tortured into such enormous, sausagelike curls—Martha could almost see it, the glimmer of a laughing, lively girl.

"I daresay I'd have quite liked you," she murmured with a twinge of remorse.

It was strange, that night, to climb into Dead Cora's bed and go to sleep. She was glad she had found out that Cora was not a peevish thing after all, for she doubted she would have slept a wink with the thought of those cross, goggly eyes watching her all night long.

The Gowrie House

Father could not stay long at Doune House.

"I shall be sorry to miss Kenneth," he said regretfully. But it could not be helped. He intended to make a short visit to her brothers' school on the other side of the city, do a bit of trading in the market, and then return home quickly. He did not like to spend many days away from the estate at this time of year.

"Be a good lass, now," he told Martha, "and mind your manners. Your mither will be expecting to hear from you at least twice a week—see you dinna disappoint her."

Martha promised, stifling a sigh. She wished people would stop telling her to mind her manners. She kissed Father good-bye. When he climbed into the carriage, she felt a pang of regret that their journey together was over. They had been alone in the carriage for so many hours, but they had not talked and talked as Martha had imagined they might.

But there was little time to think about it, for Sim cracked the reins and the carriage rolled away. Father's hand waved out the window, and then it was gone, and Martha felt that this was the real beginning of her visit to Perth.

Father need not have worried that she would neglect to write her mother, for she missed Mum dreadfully and had little bits of letters writing themselves in her head all through the day. Everything she saw, she wanted to tell to Mum. She had written her a long letter the night before by candlelight at Cora's little writing table, telling her all about the journey, and

Grisie's fine house, and Cora herself. Near the bottom of the paper she had had to write extremely small in order to fit in all the messages that must be sent to Cook and Auld Mary and the cousins at Fairlie. Looking the letter over afterward, Martha had been rather relieved that Miss Crow was away from Glencaraid and would therefore not see this rather smudgy epistle. Miss Crow never scolded for poor penmanship, but she did tease.

It was going to be difficult, because there was so much to tell. Doune House was a place completely unlike Martha's home. It was hushed and grave, haughtily holding itself aloof from the noisy street outside its walls. Martha had counted at least six servants in the house, but they went about their work so invisibly that she could not have said for certain that there were not more servants she simply had not met yet. She had the queer sensation that every time she entered a room, someone had just slipped out through another door. Certain rooms were forbidden to her at certain times of the day, so that the maidservants might do their dusting and polishing undisturbed.

It took her three entire days to discover the name of the gentle housemaid who filled her water jug, made her bed, and emptied her chamber pot. Jennie, for that was her name, seemed reluctant to speak to Martha, though she smiled warmly whenever Martha spoke to her. There was Kitty, of course, and the footman, John, who had shown Father to his room the day they arrived. He took no notice of Martha whatsoever, and the butler, Simmons, maintained a cordial silence in her presence. Somewhere in the house there was a kitchen and presumably a cook, but Martha had never seen her, nor the kitchenmaid either.

Jennie and Kitty carried in trays of food at the appropriate times, and they returned later to carry the empty dishes away. Sometimes at dinner, Mr. MacDougal would be talking while Kitty carried a dish of food around the table, serving, and he talked right through her as she bent to slip a plate of this or that before him, as if she were not even there.

No wonder she scowls so, thought Martha. She

would hate to be talked through as if she were nothing but air.

Every morning after breakfast, Grisie took Martha into the drawing room, where there was a large, beautiful pianoforte. Martha liked to hear Grisie play. But Grisie made *her* play, too, urging her to sit straighter, curve her fingers properly, and repeat phrase after difficult phrase. Martha grumbled about it, but her complaints stemmed more from habit than from an actual dislike of Grisie's lessons. Martha had never liked to practice her music, and so of course she must chafe under Grisie's instruction; but the truth was that she was actually enjoying the instrument for the first time since its novelty had worn off a few months after Father had brought one into their own home. Grisie was a patient, relentless teacher. She did not sigh over Martha's mistakes or make mocking comments, as she had once been wont to do; now she was unfailingly gentle and soft-voiced. But she required Martha to repeat passages over and over again, until Martha could play them without stumbling.

Sometimes Martha felt as if she were in a dream, her sister was such a strange combination of Grisie and not-Grisie.

On fine days, they went out walking or made calls on neighbors. Sometimes Grisie took Martha along the Watergate Street toward the river. Grisie had to hold her skirts above the grime of the road, picking her way gingerly around the horse droppings. Martha was more glad than ever that her skirts did not yet quite reach her ankles. She had not expected the city to be so dirty. She had imagined it would be grand and fine, like the interior of Doune House.

The river, though, was not dirty. It was beautiful. The first time Martha saw the bridge over the Tay, it took her breath away. It was a wide, flat, stone road set upon graceful stone arches, a structure somehow mighty and delicate all at once. Martha could not imagine how such a thing might have been built. The river was a great deal wider than she had expected. The bridge's wide arches were tall enough for small craft to sail beneath.

"Of course the view from our own garden is much finer," said Grisie. "But I thought you'd like to see the bridge up close."

"Aye," said Martha. "Grisie, how did they build the middle part?"

Grisie shrugged. "Alisdair would ken, I doubt not."

"Where *is* the boys' school?" Martha asked. It was strange to be in the same city as her brothers and never see them.

"Och, it's away across town there," said Grisie, pointing westward.

"I wish we could go and see them."

"You'll see them soon," Grisie said. "Come, let's go back."

On the way home, they made a detour, for Grisie wanted to stop at a stationers'. She bought a bottle of ink for fourpence. As they were leaving, they encountered a woman entering the shop. She wore the largest, most fearfully ornamented hat Martha had ever seen. The woman bestowed upon Grisie a beaming smile.

"Mrs. MacDougal, my dear! How splendid to meet you here!"

Grisie greeted her with equal delight.

"Martha, come and meet Mrs. Halliwell! My wee sister, come for a visit," she explained to the lady in the enormous hat, which Martha thought resembled a gorse bush stuck all over with feathers. Mrs. Halliwell cooed over Martha, patting her head as if she were a child of three or four years old. She began talking animatedly of people Martha did not know. Martha waited as patiently as she could, watching wagons and people go by on the street. A soldier passed on horseback, his red coat bright as rowanberries. He reined his steed before the largest house in the Watergate Street. A tall stone arch opened off the street, through which Martha could glimpse a flagged courtyard leading to another stone wall. The house towered above the arch, taller than the treetops that hinted at a garden behind the wall. Martha counted at least four chimneys, and more than a dozen windows on the south side of the house alone.

That evening, at tea, while Mr. MacDougal read his newspaper and ate his biscuits in

Evening

silence, Martha asked Grisie about the house. "Who lives there? Like a palace, it was."

Grisie nodded. "Och, aye, it used to belong to the Earl of Gowrie. Dinna you mind the story? I ken I'd heard it long before I came here."

Martha shook her head.

"Och, well then." Grisie put down her teacup, her eyes lively. She looked like Mum. "'Tis a tale o' murder and intrigue. No man alive kens the truth o' what happened there, that bitter night in the year 1600."

"What, what?" Martha cried. Mr. MacDougal lowered a corner of his paper and peered at her with one eye. Martha ducked her head apologetically. She had not meant to be loud.

Grisie went on, her voice softer. "Well, what happened was this. 'Twas in August o' that year that King James the Sixth came to pay the Earl o' Gowrie a visit. There was a scuffle in the night—swords clashin', men cryin' out—and in the morning, the earl and his brother lay dead. 'Twas said they had plotted against the king's life, but the assassination failed and they were killed by the king's guard. But others whispered that the plotting had been on the king's part, and he had only made it out to look as if the earl had betrayed him. No one kens what truly happened. One o' Scotland's greatest mysteries, it is. Would but that the walls could speak, or the blood that fell upon the stones . . ."

The newspaper came down again. This time it was Grisie whom Mr. MacDougal eyed askance, but he said nothing. Grisie bit her lip and hastily picked up her tea.

Martha shivered, imagining the gruesome scene. She ached to know what had really gone on inside the Gowrie House that night. It was unthinkable that the truth had never come out, that no one knew whether the king was betrayed or betrayer. Was the Earl of Gowrie a scoundrel who deserved his fate, or had he been cruelly murdered in his own home?

"Who lives there now?" she asked. She could scarcely imagine sleeping in such a house. Its secrets would torment her. But

Grisie said only soldiers lived in the Gowrie House nowadays. It had been a barracks for many years.

"Why would the king make a plot like that?" she asked. "He'd have had to be very wicked, having someone killed and making it look as if they were the ones in the wrong. Was he a wicked king? Or do you think 'twas the other way round? But why would the earl and his brother want the king dead? And him a guest under the earl's own roof!"

Down came Mr. MacDougal's paper once more, with an impatient rattle.

"Perhaps," he said shortly, "he was the sort of person who drove his host mad wi' ceaseless chatter."

Martha snapped her mouth shut. She stared at Mr. MacDougal in surprise, but he seemed not to notice, disappearing behind his paper once more. Martha shot a glance at Grisie, whose brow was furrowed in what might have been embarrassment or anger, Martha couldn't tell. But when Grisie looked up and caught her eye, a pulse of understanding passed between them. Grisie smiled, ever so slightly. Martha grinned and had to snatch up her teacup lest a laugh burst out of her.

In that silent glancing moment, something shifted between them. It was a hidden thing, like the mystery of the Gowrie House. Nothing was different on the outside to explain what had happened within—but something had happened, some important, mysterious act. Martha could not put it into words, but she felt it. Grisie had ceased to be "my elder sister"—she was now simply "my sister," and Martha loved her more than she had ever thought possible.

Sisters

There came a stretch of bad weather, chill rainy days when water ran in rivulets down the paved streets. Martha thought of the hayfields at home and hoped the weather there was not so grim. She stared out the dripping windows, wondering where all the street children had gone, and the roaming dogs. Where were their homes? Did they have homes? Were they huddled somewhere in a corner, vainly trying to stay dry? She was of a mind to invite them in, if anyone was there. She went through the hall and opened the front door, looking out, but the street was deserted. Not even the rats would venture out in such a downpour. Kitty came into the passage—it always did seem to be Kitty who caught her doing things she ought not to be doing—and scolded her for letting in the rain.

"Spoil the master's clean floors, ye will," she muttered under her breath.

"Och, I'm sorry!" Martha cried, noticing for the first time how the rain was spattering in at her feet. "Shall I fetch a towel?"

"Ye!" Kitty seemed shocked by the notion. "Nay, nay, I'll take care o't. Ye go on—her ladyship's wantin' ye."

On the wet days, Grisie liked to keep to her pretty sitting room, with a lively little fire glowing on the hearth. She sat in her favorite chair, working at her needlepoint, while Martha sat upon the hearthrug with her arms around her knees, the two of them talking as they had never talked before. Martha felt a soaring kind of joy to have such conversations with her sister, who had always treated her like a little child. Perhaps it was because Grisie missed her family, her old home, or perhaps it was because Martha really was older; but the old bickering habits had fallen away from them.

They talked about home, about Mum and Cook and Sandy and the cousins at Fairlie. Martha told Grisie about seeing Mr. Gow in Crieff, how Father had suspected him of poaching and had not even been surprised. Grisie was not surprised either. She said everyone in Glencaraid knew that Gow was a scoundrel, and the only reason Father did not turn him off the land was out of compassion for Mrs. Gow and the children.

"My father-in-law would have seen him turned out ages agc," she said. "He'd not trouble himself about the man's family—he'd say it was their business to worry about themselves."

Martha shuddered, thinking of kind Mrs. Gow and sweet-faced Sorcha, of little Ranald and the baby. It was not their fault Mr. Gow was shiftless.

"I'm glad our father is the way he is," she said passionately. She was fiercely proud of Father. He was very, very busy; he was strict and stern. Sometimes it seemed his thoughts spoke louder to him than the person sitting opposite him in a carriage. "He's good and kind and just. He cares about people . . . even if he doesn't laugh with them the way Uncle Harry does," she added reflectively.

"That's why he loves Mother so," said Grisie. "She's so merry, it does him good. And he kens it. She keeps him from being too solemn."

"Is that why you love Ken?" Martha asked. "He's merry. You used to be cross all the time, but you're not anymore."

Grisie laughed. "I? Cross? It's a wonder I wasna a great deal crosser, the way you used to plague the life out o' me. Do you mind the time you ruined my new white muslin frock? Nay, you'd be too young to remember."

"Did I really?"

"Aye, it was just made; I'd not yet worn it. Ten years old, I was, and you were a wee thing o' two. You got into Mum's jam closet—that was naughty enough all on its own—and then when you'd eaten half a jar o' her best plum preserves, you went into the nursery and climbed right into the clothespress. You pulled my frock off the peg and wiped your jammy hands all over it. Mum had to dye the frock purple, in the end."

Martha was embarrassed, but she could not help laughing. She loved when Grisie told about things that had happened so long ago, she could not remember them. It was strange to think there were things about her own life that Grisie remembered better than she did.

"Do you remember when I was born, Grisie?" she asked.

Grisie nodded, a little secretive smile lighting her face.

"You were the sweetest wee thing," she said softly. "The prettiest bairn I'd ever seen. I was too young to remember when Alisdair and Robbie were born. I mind when Duncan was, and I thought his head looked just like a shriveled old turnip." She giggled. "He improved, o' course. But just at first I thought he was the ugliest thing I'd ever seen. But you—you were smooth and pink and sweet. I was so glad you were a girl. Prayed and prayed for a sister, I had. I told Mother that I was very sorry, but I couldna love my brothers anymore because I would have to use all my love up on you."

Martha grinned in delight. "What did she say?"

"She laughed and said that that was the fine thing about love—you couldna run out. It's like the loaves and fishes, she said. The more you pass around, the more you have left over."

An Organ-grinder's Monkey

Martha did not see much of Mr. MacDougal. He breakfasted in his chamber; he nearly always dined elsewhere; and although most evenings he took his tea in the parlor with the two sisters, he was nearly always shrouded behind his paper. He seldom spoke to Martha. Sometimes she wondered if he even remembered her name.

One terrible afternoon, he entered the parlor

just as Martha was stepping down from a chair. She had climbed onto it to look at the picture of the white-gowned woman above the fireplace. She had an idea it was a portrait of Mrs. MacDougal, Kenneth and Dead Cora's mother, whom Martha had met at Glencaraid; but it was hung too high for her to be sure. She had been careful to slip off her shoes before stepping onto the chair, but Mr. MacDougal reacted as if she had smeared mud upon the seat and rubbed it well in. His eyes blazed, and he outright yelled at her to get down this instant—which of course she had been already in the process of doing.

"I beg your pardon, sir!" Martha gasped, fumbling for her shoes. "I was only looking—"

"I ken what ye were aboot!" the old man roared, his wig quivering. "Climbing on the furniture like an organ-grinder's monkey!"

"Nay, sir, I was—"

Again he cut her off.

"In my day, lassie, children knew better than to contradict their elders."

"I wasna contradicting—" Martha cried, and

then she bit her lip, because that *was* contra-dicting.

Mr. MacDougal huffed air through his nose and, taking hold of her upper arm, shoved her toward the door.

"Go along to yer chamber, child. Ye'll have your tea alone this night. I shall have a word wi' your sister aboot this. If ye were my child, I'd take a cane to ye."

Martha went, fuming, the harsh words stinging her ears. She did not want Mr. MacDougal to think poorly of her parents, or to suppose they raised ill-mannered children.

"He wouldna listen!" she cried to Grisie later that night. "It isna fair! He's a horrid auld man, he is. He wasna like this when Father was here."

"Hush!" murmured Grisie. "He'll hear you. You ought to have kenned better, Martha, than to have climbed upon the furniture in the first place."

"Grisie!" Martha wailed in dismay, astonished that her sister should take old Balliecruin's part.

"Whisht, I'm not saying he was in the right, dearest! Only that you ought to have thought before you—"

She broke off, squeezing Martha close. "Hush now, let's not let such a trifle spoil our nice visit. I've had a letter from Kenneth; he ought to be home tomorrow, if all goes well."

Martha wiped her eyes, determined that Mr. MacDougal would not make her cry. But she could not help adding bitterly, "He would nivver have shouted so if Father'd been here."

"Aye, and you'd nivver have climbed on a chair in the first place," Grisie pointed out.

Martha could not deny there was some truth to that.

Kenneth

Martha had been at Doune House for more than a fortnight before Kenneth returned home. She was looking out her window, watching a white-capped woman who she guessed must be the cook buying eels from one of the fishwives who walked up and down the street each day, bent beneath the large baskets of fish they carried on their backs. A horse came trotting up the street, a fine bay mare, and its rider reined to a stop directly in front of Doune House. Martha heard the cook cry out in delight, and the driver jumped lightly down from the saddle, his green tailcoat swinging jauntily. He turned, and Martha could see that it was her brother-in-law.

"Kenneth!" she cried, waving through the glass. He must have heard her, for he looked up and broke into a wide grin when his gaze reached her window.

"Why, 'tis Juliet!" he cried, his voice ringing through the glass. Martha laughed. Kenneth was just the teasing sort of person she liked best. He knew that she was reading the plays of Shakespeare with Miss Crow at home, and whenever Grisie sent a letter to Martha at Glencaraid, Kenneth would add a postscript jokingly addressed to "Lady MacBeth" or "Cordelia."

He called now: "But soft, what light through yonder window breaks? Except I suppose in your case, it's more apt to be the *window* that breaks, isn't it? How fare you, sister? Upset any ale stoups of late?"

Martha winced, remembering how she had knocked over a mug of ale at Grisie and

Kenneth's wedding supper, soaking her own mother's new silk gown. She had successfully avoided thinking of that for months.

Kenneth had given his horse to a servant who appeared on the street through some entrance other than the main door, which was directly below Martha's window. *Seven*, she thought, adding the groomsman to her private tally. Kenneth bounded down the three narrow steps to the front door and passed out of Martha's view. She turned away from the window and hurried downstairs, calling to Grisie as she ran.

"Kenneth's home!"

"Hush, girl! Nae need to bellow!" came Mr. MacDougal's stern growl from the parlor.

Martha winced again, furious with herself for annoying Balliecruin once more. But she forgot all about it when Kenneth strode into the passage, grinning his warm, brotherly grin.

"I beg your pardon, miss; I was looking for my wee sister-in-law," he said. "But I see there's no one here but your ladyship."

"Dinna be daft, Kenneth, 'tis I." Martha laughed.

"Why, so it is! Bless me, Miss Martha, you're that grown up, I hardly recognized you!"

"Dearest!" Grisie swept down the stairs, her eyes shining. Kenneth caught her up in his arms and kissed her. Martha looked away, embarrassed.

"How I've missed you!"

"Not half so much as I've missed you. Are you—well?" he asked.

"Aye, indeed, quite as well as we hoped." Grisie's cheeks flushed red.

"When were you ill?" asked Martha in frank surprise. Grisie had seemed perfectly healthy since the day Martha arrived in Perth.

Kenneth laughed. "Dinna worrit yourself, Miss Martha. 'Tis a husband's privilege to cosset his wife."

Mr. MacDougal's voice came roaring from the parlor. "Well, lad, d'ye intend to stand in the passage yammering all day, or will ye come and greet your father!"

Kenneth's eyebrows went up. "Och, he's in a fine state," he whispered. "What've you been doing to irk the auld man, Martha?"

Martha began to sputter, but Kenneth winked and she saw that he was teasing again. He escorted Grisie into the parlor. Martha started to follow them, but thinking better of it, she slipped back up to her room. She'd had enough of Mr. MacDougal.

Doune House was a great deal merrier with Kenneth at home. He whistled in the passage and joked with the servants. Martha even saw him set Kitty laughing with one of his jests. He too liked to read his newspaper at teatime, but he was always calling out interesting bits of news to Grisie and Martha. Mr. MacDougal glowered at him from over the top of his own paper, but he never said a word. It was impossible to be angry at Kenneth, thought Martha, even for short-tempered Balliecruin.

In this she was mistaken, though, as she learned a few days after Kenneth's arrival. She approached the parlor one morning to hear Mr. MacDougal shouting at someone in his most searing manner.

"The greatest piece o' foolishness I ivver

heard tell o'! Namby-pamby, cowardly, simple-minded foolishness!"

"Cowardly!" Ken's outraged voice made the chandelier rattle. "You're a fine one to talk, sending me to do your dirty work! You ought to have told me in the first place what you were sending me to do—I'd not have gone at all. I'll not be a party to it, Father, rousting honest, hardworking tenants from their homes. And for what? Money, always money. I dinna care if there's twice as much to be made in sheep farming. If you wanted the land cleared, then you ought to have gone and done it yourself."

"Aye, the more fool me, for believing I could trust my son to respect his father's wishes!"

Martha was frozen. She had never heard a father and son speak to each other like that. She did not think she had ever heard *anyone* speak so harshly. She could not remotely imagine her own father speaking to one of her brothers in such a manner. She shrank away from the parlor door, hoping the quarrelers would not know she had heard them.

"Watch it!" growled a voice, and she wheeled around to see Kitty standing behind her with a tray of scones. "For shame," the servant whispered, "listening at keyholes!"

"I nivver!" cried Martha in outrage. The voices inside fell abruptly silent. For a long moment Martha and Kitty stared at each other in the awful silence. Then the voices began again, rumbling low and indistinct. Martha flew up the stairs to her room, not caring what Kitty thought.

Cora gazed at her reproachfully from her dainty table.

"Dinna look at me so," said Martha. "He's not *my* father. Thank the Lord!"

The Dead Palsy

Nothing was ever said in Martha's presence of the disagreement between Kenneth and his father. It seemed to have been patched up, for that evening at tea Kenneth spoke to his father with deference and courtesy, and Mr. MacDougal barked no more than usual. Martha kept out of his way as much as possible.

One day the MacDougals were invited to dine with Mrs. Halliwell, and Grisie said Martha had been included in the party.

"You'll wear your yellow silk," she said

eagerly. "Och, I do wish Mum had made your skirt a wee bit longer."

"It's almost to me ankles already!" cried Martha incredulously.

Grisie made her sit in a chair to have her hair dressed by Jennie, under Grisie's supervision. Martha gritted her teeth, trying not to scream as her unruly curls were tortured into ringlets smooth and regular enough to satisfy Grisie's critical eye. The yellow silk was slipped on, its buttons buttoned, its sash tied and retied, its gauzy embroidered collar smoothed into place.

"There," pronounced Grisie with approval. "Lovely."

She sent Martha down to the parlor to wait until the others were ready.

" 'Twill be hours yet," Martha moaned, for Grisie's own hair had not yet been dressed.

"Hush. Go and practice your music," Grisie ordered.

Martha went to the drawing room, but she had played no more than half a melody when

Mr. MacDougal stuck his head in, frowning.

"There's ruckus enough in this hoose today wi'oot your help," he growled. He had a headache and had told Kenneth he was not going to Mrs. Halliwell's. "Go along ootside, child, and wait in the garden till ye're called."

Obediently, Martha went. It had rained the night before, so the grass was wet, and the stone benches that stood at the river end of the garden were beaded with water. Martha sighed. She could not sit, and she hardly dared walk on the damp grass, for fear she would splatter her shoes and invoke Grisie's wrath. Grisie took dining out extremely seriously.

She kept instead to the path along the shrubbery. At intervals along the neatly trimmed hedge, bushes had been clipped to resemble animals of one kind or another. The quaint figures always delighted her. She went eagerly down the path looking for the next creature: a lion; a bear; a deer; something that appeared to be a dog standing on its hind legs, but that Martha guessed was meant to be a rearing horse. The path turned a sharp corner, and Martha, hurrying around the curve, strayed off the path. Her feet hit the wet grass and slid out from beneath her, and she found herself sitting on the damp ground.

It was not a serious fall. She scrambled to her feet, not the least bit hurt. The yellow silk, however, was not as fortunate. It was now a yellow silk with a wide wet splotch on the back and grass stains on the elbows. Even just peering over her shoulder, Martha could see the damage to the back of the frock.

She stood there a moment, postponing the unpleasantness that was sure to follow. Then, taking a breath, she trudged inside and went straight to her sister's room.

"Och, Martha!" cried Grisie in dismay. "Look at you—you're like a sheep in the mud season! How shall I take you now? You ken your striped linen is soaking in the laundry tub this blessed minute. The muslin will not suit at all for a formal dinner. How could you?"

"I didna do it on purpose," said Martha

indignantly. "I slipped."

Grisie sighed. "Happen so, but you'd no business—"

"But—but—" sputtered Martha. "Mr. MacDougal *made* me go outside! 'Tis no my fault the paths are muddy!"

"You might have taken care not to—"

"Hush, wife," interrupted Kenneth. "It canna be helped now."

"She'll have to stay home," said Grisie unhappily. "I suppose I ought to stay with you—"

But Martha could see Grisie wanted to go. "I dinna mind being alone," she assured her sister. "I shall write a letter to Mum."

Grisie was not happy, but in the end it was settled just as Martha suggested. Kitty came in to announce that the carriage was ready. Grisie, jerking on her gloves, told Martha to change her clothes and mind her manners, not to trouble Mr. MacDougal, and to eat her soup without slurping. Martha gritted her teeth and promised to be good.

After they were gone, she went into the

parlor to begin her letter to Mum. Mr. MacDougal came in a short while later, glanced at her with pursed lips, and settled into his favorite chair with a fat leather-bound book. Martha wrote on, taking great care not to let her pen scratch too loudly on the paper. She had never been alone with Mr. MacDougal before, and she shuddered to think of making him angry with her without Grisie there.

One moment old Balliecruin was sitting in his chair, frowning over the pages of his book, and the next moment he had pitched suddenly forward onto the floor. Martha looked at him in astonishment. For a fleeting second she had the wild idea that he had seen a mouse and had dived out of his chair to catch it. Then she saw that he was lying on the floor, the book splayed beneath him, his eyes half closed, his mouth open. His skin was a sickly gray color. He was shaking, twitching, his hands reaching out to clutch empty air. Martha stood frozen, staring at him. She knew she must do something, but she could not think what. The only thought of any sort that came into her head was *Do something.* In itself this was not the least bit helpful.

"Sir," she faltered. "Mr. MacDougal, sir!" At last her limbs unfroze and she knelt beside him. But she hardly dared touch him. His twitching frightened her more than she had ever been frightened in her life.

"Sir!" she cried again, louder, tremulously touching his chest, his dull gray face. His heavy eyes stared unseeingly past her. "Jennie! Someone! Och, do please someone help!"

She did not know how to still the twitching. It seemed to her he would crack his skull if he went on dashing it against the floor in this way, so she put her hands beneath his head, trying to still it. His wig had slipped awry, covering one of the staring eyes. Gulping a little, she lifted it off his head, half expecting him to rise up and roar at her with a "What the de'il do ye think ye're doing, lass?" It seemed a terribly impertinent thing to do.

But Balliecruin did not respond. Martha thought—she could not be sure—that the twitching was subsiding a bit. *Oh please, please,* she prayed silently, *help*.

Then she shouted again.

"HELP! HELP! HELP!"

After what seemed like an age, someone did come. Kitty strode into the room, talking to herself in an outraged tone.

"What's the lass gone and done now! She's broken the chandelier, I ken it— Lord ha' mercy!"

She stopped short, her eyes wide with shock.

"Saints preserve us! What's happened?"

Martha looked pleadingly up at her. "He just fell over, he did, and he willna stop shaking, and I dinna ken what to do!"

"Steady his head—there. Have ye a hankie? Good, give it me." She stuffed Martha's handkerchief into the old man's mouth. "Noo he'll no bite his tongue off, God willin'. Ye bide just like that, child; I'll go for a doctor."

Kitty rushed out, and Martha heard her barking orders to the other servants. The front door opened and closed with a bang. Jennie came running in, with Simmons on her heels, and suddenly the room was full of people: all the quiet, invisible servants Martha had only glimpsed before. Someone put a cushion beneath Mr. MacDougal's head, and someone else covered him with a blanket. A hand touched Martha's shoulder, and Jennie's gentle voice told her to run along to her chamber.

"The doctor'll set him to rights, miss. It's lucky ye were here; who kens how long he might ha' lain there otherwise? Go on, noo, and I'll bring ye a cup o' tea."

Numbly, Martha rose to her feet. She went slowly to her bedchamber and sank into one of the chintz-covered chairs. Dead Cora stared at her from the table. Martha looked away. Mr. MacDougal was Cora's father; suddenly Martha was very conscious of all the times she had had complaining thoughts about the old man.

It was horrible to sit alone in the still room, waiting, wondering, not knowing if Mr. MacDougal was alive or dead. Footsteps thundered up and down the passages; voices sometimes rumbled and sometimes shouted, indistinctly, urgently. Doors opened, doors closed. Someone was crying—Martha could not tell who. She felt half crazed with questions and fear. Jennie must have forgotten the promised cup of tea, for she never returned.

Mrs. Dabble

Dinnertime came and went while Martha waited alone in her room, forgotten. Her stomach ached with worry and hunger—the latter gradually overtaking the former. Every moment she was expecting Jennie to appear in the doorway with a tray of something nice to eat. Bread and jam, perhaps, or currant cakes, or pickled herring and some of the fine Doune House cheese. At last she could stand it no longer. She opened her door and looked down the deserted hall, listening to the murmur of noises from Mr. MacDougal's rooms downstairs.

The upper story was quiet as a graveyard. Her stomach growled. She made up her mind—she would slip down the back stairs and find the kitchen, and she would ask the cook very politely if she might have a bit of bread and cheese. She hoped that the cook was a friendly sort of person, and that Kitty would be nowhere near.

The kitchen was not difficult to find, once she had located the servants' staircase. She crept down the steps, feeling her way down with the tips of her toes, her hand sliding along the wall. It was the darkest, steepest staircase she had ever gone down—steeper than the hills that surrounded Loch Caraid, she thought. As she reached the lowest steps, she could hear sounds of dishes clinking and a spoon scraping an iron pan, sounds she would know with her eyes closed. It seemed that the kitchen opened right off the back staircase.

She hesitated on the steps, listening. Servants were talking; she heard the voice of John, the footman, and a crisp, thin voice she did not recognize.

"It's the dead palsy, it is. I doubt the auld master'll ivver be himself again." That was John.

"Och, and him sae hale and hearty. A terrible shame it is, that's what I say. Ah, me, there's naught we can do for him noo but pray."

"Ha!" That was Kitty. Her scornful tones were unmistakable. "An' change his beddin', an' feed 'im broth, and wash 'im—ayc, there's naught for the doctor to do, but us'll have ourselves a fine lot o' work lookin' after t'auld man now."

"Kitty!" The crisp voice was even crisper. "How can ye say such a thing!"

Martha felt cold all over. She did not know what the dead palsy was, but it must be dreadful, if Mr. MacDougal would never be himself again—if he would need servants to feed him and wash him, as if he were a baby. She wished Auld Mary were here—she could cure any illness.

She could hear Kitty sniffing in an offended manner. "I'm sure I didna mean to upset ye, Mrs. Dabble. I didna ken ye had such an affection for t'auld man. Sure and many's the time I've heard ye gripin' aboot him."

"Shut yer mouth, Kitty, ye spiteful auld cat," cried John.

There was a brief silence. Then: "I'll no forget that," said Kitty icily, and suddenly she came through the doorway to where Martha was standing. She stopped short, her eyes wide.

"Ye!" she cried. "Spyin' again, are ye? Ye're a bad lass and no mistakin'!"

"Nay!" Martha sputtered. "I didna mean— I was hungry, that's all—"

But there was not much she could say, because she *had* been eavesdropping. Her cheeks burned.

"No one brought me any dinner," she said, sounding belligerent when she did not mean to. She was ashamed of herself for listening at doorways, furious with herself for confirming Kitty's bad opinion of her.

"Selfish piece, ye are, thinkin' o' yerself when the master's lyin' on his deathbed, like as not," snapped Kitty. But the others were crowding behind her to see to whom she was talking. At the sight of Martha, John's eyebrows went up wonderingly, and a tall, bony woman in a well-starched apron stared at her with astonishment.

"The child!" she exclaimed, and her voice was the crisp one Martha had heard. Martha guessed she was Mrs. Dabble, the cook. "Lord have mercy, she's right. Sure and we forgot all about her. Not a bite to eat she's had since mornin'."

Clucking her tongue, she pushed past Kitty and stood before Martha at the bottom of the steps.

"Come here where I can have a look at ye, child," she said, taking Martha's hand and drawing her into the kitchen. Martha glimpsed a large, cluttered room with a stone fireplace and a long, high table. Her heart gave a thrum of longing for Cook's cozy, low-ceilinged kitchen at home, with the peats stacked against the wall and her dear spiky hedgehog snuffling between the flour barrels.

Mrs. Dabble reminded her of Cook a little—not in looks, for Mrs. Dabble was all bones where Cook was soft and round—but in her bossy manner and her blunt words.

"Eh! I see Kitty was right about ye—ye're all hair and freckles. I suppose yer lady mither is always after ye to wear a hat, and ye're always after forgettin'. Well, ye'll rue that one day, when yer complexion's spoilt." She smiled, shaking her head. "Noo, then, I ken ye're hungry. I'll fix ye a tray. Run along back to yer room, now—stick to the back stairs, mind, like ye came doon. There's trouble enough in this house today wi'oot naughty lasses creepin' around gettin' into mischief. Kitty will bring yer tray right off."

Martha blinked in surprise. Mrs. Dabble had spoken so kindly that she had fully expected to stay in the kitchen.

"I'd not mind eating in here," she said hopefully. "You needna bother with a tray."

Kitty sniffed in disdain. Mrs. Dabble laughed.

"Sure and wouldn't that be a picture!" she exclaimed. "In yer nice white frock and all. Trot along, now, back upstairs where ye belong. Heaven knows I've enough on my hands this day, with the poor master put to bed and no one kennin' if he'll live or die."

The Frozen Man

Grisie came to her that evening, with red eyes. She sat on the edge of the bed and told Martha in hushed tones that Mr. MacDougal had taken a fit and slipped into a coma. The doctor had little hope of his recovery. Kenneth had sent a man to his mother at Balliecruin. Grisie expected Mrs. MacDougal to reach Doune House in three or four days.

"I suppose I'd better go back," she said. "I made Kenneth promise to lie down for a few hours' rest. Kitty is with my father-in-law now.

He canna be left alone."

If Martha had thought Doune House was quiet before, it was nothing compared to the careful silence now preserved within its walls. The servants spoke in whispers, if they spoke at all. Kenneth was pale, his eyes bleak. He did not tease or joke with Martha now. He sat for long hours beside his father's bed, leaving only because Grisie begged him to eat or sleep a little. At those times Grisie took his place beside the sickbed. A man on his deathbed must never be left to die alone. A prayerful vigil was all that could be done for the laird of Balliecruin now.

Martha ate her meals alone in her room. At teatime on the second day, Kitty came to her.

"Ye're needed," she said shortly. "Miss Grisell has gone and fainted, she has. Master Ken says she's just overspent herself and must stay in bed. But he canna leave her, and the rest o' the house is in a terrible flurry gettin' ready for her ladyship's arrival. Ye'll have to sit wi' the auld man; ye're the only one as has naught to do."

"Me!" Martha gasped.

"Aye, that's what I said," said Kitty. "Come along, then, child. Ye'll finish yer tea in the master's chamber."

"Och, nay!" cried Martha. "I mean—I'm quite full, thank you. I'll go. But Grisie—she'll be all right?"

Her head was whirling. First Mr. MacDougal, now her sister—the thought of Grisie being ill was like a hand squeezing her heart. But Kitty snorted.

"There's naught amiss wi' her that time willna cure," she said. "Go on, then! Hurry! The master must no be left alone!"

She all but pushed Martha out of her room toward the stairs. With great trepidation, Martha went down to Mr. MacDougal's chamber. She stood before the heavy oaken door, uncertain whether or not to knock. But no, there would be no one to answer. Slowly she pushed open the door.

The room was dim, almost dark. Heavy draperies shrouded the windows, and only a subdued hearthfire and candles flickering in the wall sconces brought a little light to the room. An enormous four-poster bed jutted out from the far wall. The old man lay in it, as still as death, a woven coverlet drawn up to his chin. Martha glanced at him and glanced away. There was a chair beside the bed, and a little table with a candle burning on it beside the chair. She sat down, looking everywhere but at the old man. The walls were paneled with wood of a shade so dark as to be nearly black. It might have been midnight, for all Martha could tell. It was impossible to picture the beggar children playing in the sunny street outside; and yet she could hear their shouts, now and then, through the walls. Once she heard Kitty, scolding them out the window for disturbing "t'auld master on his deathbed." *That*, at least, Martha had no difficulty picturing.

On the wall beside her hung a large tapestry. Tiny figures in quaint costumes chased each other through a wood, blowing horns, fitting arrows to slender bowstrings. No, not chasing each other after all: chasing a stag, wounded and desperate at the top of the picture, a long black arrow piercing his flank. The hunters' faces were jubilant and eager, their clothing gorgeously bright even in the darkened room. The ladies wore strange hats with gauzy veils fluttering down, or garlands of flowers upon their gleaming hair. Hounds gamboled like kittens among the tall, straight trees. They all seemed, the whole lot of them, to be flaunting their delight, as if they cared not a whit that the doctor had said Mr. MacDougal would never rise from his bed again. Only the stag, a red flower blooming against his sleek brown side, looked out upon the old man with sympathy and suffering in his eyes.

At last Martha could not help it; she followed the stag's gaze and stared at Mr. MacDougal. She had heard Kitty say the old man was shrunken, that he would soon waste away to nothing. But it did not seem that way to Martha. He was no smaller; his chin jutted out just as proudly as it always had. Only his scalp was different, for the pink skin showed through the sparse gray hair on top. She did not like seeing him without his wig. He looked less lordly, more . . . more ordinary. He reminded her of Sandy, her father's steward at home—Sandy, who had seven children whom he was always giving horse-a-back rides or bouncing on his knee. Sandy's favorite game to play with his bairns was to lie motionless on his back as if he were dead; the children would rush up to him and shake him, and poke at him, trying to rouse him, and just when they had begun to worry if perhaps their father really wasn't fooling this time, he would reach out his hands and grab their legs, roaring, and tickle them until they shrieked. Martha had seen them play this game a hundred times. She could almost imagine that Mr. MacDougal was playing it now—that if she leaned close to his motionless figure and touched him with the lightest finger tap, he would burst into life and boom at her with his sonorous voice.

She hated the thoughts that came creeping unbidden, unwelcome, into her mind. Suppose it were Sandy in this bed? Suppose one day his game should be not a game at all, but real—suppose the dead palsy should strike him as well? Suppose . . . suppose it were to happen to her own father?

Mr. MacDougal was Kenneth's father. He had had a little girl once. He was a *father*. Kenneth loved him; Mrs. MacDougal loved him. Martha felt a dull heaviness in her middle, a sick sort of ache. She had disliked Balliecruin so intensely, had thought him unjust and cold. She had thought how much nicer her visit to Perth would be if he were not around. She wished she could take it back, could unthink the thoughts. She wished she had loved him too.

"I'm sorry," she whispered.

Grisie said no one knew if Mr. MacDougal could hear what was spoken around him or not. Kitty said only a fool would believe such a statue could hear. It was awful to think about—that the old man might lie there forever not seeing or talking, hearing nothing, knowing nothing.

"Can you hear me?" she whispered, and the

sound of her voice in the silent room made her shrink back into her chair. She did not feel like herself at all. The Martha Morse who boated upon Loch Caraid and climbed the stone wall atop the Creag seemed like someone else, someone she had known a long time ago. She felt a sudden terrible wave of homesickness. She wondered if Cook had put up all the blackberry preserves already. Somehow she could not bear the thought of this chore being finished without her.

"I want to go home," she told Mr. MacDougal.

If he heard her, he showed no sign.

"Please dinna die," she whispered.

She wanted, a little, to shake him, to shout in his ear. It seemed as if he *must* wake up if only someone were to shout loud enough. How was it possible that no one, not even the doctor, knew whether his mind was alive?

Empty Shell

On the fourth day, Mrs. MacDougal arrived. Martha had only a glimpse of her from the drawing-room window as the tall, slender lady alit from her carriage. With one gloved hand, she clutched the folds of a knitted shawl over the bodice of her sober gray linen gown. Kenneth came rushing out the door and put his arms around her. She seemed to crumple into him. They stood that way a moment, a sorrowful tableau on the noisy street. Supporting her elbow, Kenneth ushered her inside. Martha felt the door shut and heard their footsteps going down the passage to Mr. MacDougal's room.

She was tired of hearing everything through a wall. She had been told to keep quiet, out of the way. Grisie was resting. Martha eyed the pianoforte, feeling for once that she'd like to practice. She didn't understand why it was so important to keep the house in a state of perfect silence anyway—perhaps a great lolloping noise might be just the thing to rouse Mr. MacDougal out of his ceaseless sleep. She had half a mind to try it, just to see what would happen. But suppose it startled him so that his heart stopped? She had better not. Sighing, she turned away and went to her room to write a letter to Miss Crow instead.

The next morning when Martha awoke, Jennie was waiting for her with the news that Mr. MacDougal had died during the night. Martha stared, finding no words, not believing it. All along she had believed, underneath everything, that he would recover.

"It canna be true," she said.

Jennie's eyes were red. She swallowed, looking at the floor.

"It is, miss," she whispered. "T'auld laird has gone to his rest, and Mr. Kenneth is Balliecruin now."

Martha head was whirling. She could not think of anything in particular; as she went about the work of getting dressed, her mind grasped stupidly at words like *buttons* and *sash*. She felt dull and heavy as a blacksmith's hammer. She brushed her hair, washed her face, ate her porridge. She dreaded to leave her room. She did not want to see Mr. MacDougal—truly an empty shell now. The part of him that was really *him* had gone away.

She was taken in to see him that afternoon. Grisie held her hand, squeezing. Mrs. MacDougal sat beside the bed, dressed in black, crumpling a handkerchief in her hands. On the wall behind her, the mirror had been covered with a sheet of white linen.

"Dear child," Mrs. MacDougal said softly, reaching out a gloved hand to touch Martha's cheek. She turned her head toward the bed.

"He is at his peace now."

Slowly Martha looked. Her breath caught in her throat—he had great round staring eyes, flat eyes, a terrible glinting gray color. Gasping, she stumbled backward a step. Then she saw that they were not eyes; they were coins, one new silver coin placed over each closed eye. She swallowed, feeling foolish. She knew about putting coins on a dead person's eyes. But she had never seen a dead body before.

The grown-ups were talking in hushed voices around her. She stood there, staring, waiting. She remembered how Mr. MacDougal had barked at her about standing on the chair, and how he had twitted Grisie about her fondness for frippery. She remembered how he had shouted at Kenneth. Almost angrily, she shook her head, feeling it was all wrong that she should remember only bad things about Mr. MacDougal. It was the same as Cora being trapped forever in the image of the cross, disagreeable girl in the painting. It was not right. You could not tell from looking at the painting what sort of girl Cora had been, really.

You could not tell, now, from looking at Mr. MacDougal whether he had been a cruel person or a kind one. It was like looking at the Gowrie House: There was no way to know the truth of what had gone on inside. Only God could know the truth. Only God could see the real person, not the painting, not the empty shell.

"Come, Martha," Grisie murmured, and she was led back out of the room.

That was the last time she saw Mr. MacDougal. The next morning, his body was laid in a coffin, and the coffin was put onto a wagon. The old laird must be taken back to his estate, to be laid to rest on his own land.

The Journey Home

Mrs. MacDougal went with her husband, and so did Kenneth and Grisie. To Martha's horror, she was told she must remain at Doune House alone for a few days, until her brothers' school holidays began. They were to travel back to Glencaraid together.

"It isna *really* alone, you ken," said Grisie, her voice trembling. "Kitty will look after you."

Martha grimaced, knowing how unenthusiastic Kitty was likely to be about that idea.

Grisie's eyes overflowed, and she threw her

arms around Martha, weeping.

"Och, you've no idea how much I'll miss you!" She stepped back, wiped her eyes, and managed a weak smile. "But Martha, only guess. We're quitting Perth, Kenneth and I. And his mother, of course. We shall all remain at Balliecruin. It belongs to Kenneth now—how strange it is to think of it. Just imagine, we'll be scarcely twenty miles from home!"

She put her arms around Martha and hugged tight.

The three days of waiting for her brothers to arrive were the longest three days of Martha's life. There was a terrible ache inside her, a yearning for home so strong, she sometimes felt she could not breathe past it. She was a little angry that Grisie had not taken her to Balliecruin in the carriage. Father could have come for her on his horse. She supposed Father and Mum would go to Mr. MacDougal's funeral, anyway. But there had been no room in the carriage for Martha, for Mrs. MacDougal's lady's maid had traveled to Perth with her and must return to Balliecruin. The carriage would not comfortably hold a fifth person.

Kitty had been told to look after Martha. She seemed to regard her duty as consisting of serving Martha's meals and removing the dishes afterward. She carried out these tasks in silence, so that Martha began to feel *she* was the invisible one in the house. No one, not even Jennie, came to talk to her or see how she was getting along. She felt crazed with boredom. Grisie had told her she must not go out walking alone, and Kitty had informed her she must keep out of the garden, "to save me havin' to spend half the day cleanin' mud off the floors." Martha could hear the servants talking and laughing together from their part of the house, and she longed to be a part of it.

After a day of wandering from room to room hoping someone would remember that she was all alone and invite her down to the kitchen for a cup of tea, she made up her mind to take matters into her own hands. She went boldly down the back stairs and marched into the kitchen, prepared to withstand any uproar that might result. She was not afraid of making them angry with her—at least that would be better than being ignored or forgotten.

There was no uproar. Mrs. Dabble broke off something she was saying to Simmons, the butler, to cast an amused eye upon Martha and tell her, "Wondered when ye'd come a-huntin', I did. Hungry, are ye?"

"Er—nay—I mean, aye," faltered Martha, taken aback. She was not really hungry for anything but companionship, but she liked the thought of sitting at the worktable over a plate of cookies and milk, as she had so often done at home.

Mrs. Dabble nodded. "O' course ye are. Here, I've some nice bannocks and new honey. There ye are—mind ye dinna scatter crumbs on Kitty's precious floors, noo, and keep to the back parlor. Noo then, Mr. Simmons, as I was saying . . ."

Martha stood holding the plate Mrs. Dabble had given her, more taken aback than ever. The cook went on talking to the butler as if Martha had already left the room. Finally she did leave, fighting a lump in her throat that wanted to rise up and burst out of her. She could not eat a bit of the bannocks. When no one was looking, she slipped out the front door and gave them to a dirty, ragged little boy on the street. Even he did not stop to talk to her; he snatched up the bannocks with a glad "Thank'ee, miss!" and ran off down the street.

At last the third day came. Kitty woke Martha early and bustled her into her traveling clothes, and Simmons bustled her out the door and down the street, to where a post chaise was standing ready to depart. It was a large black carriage pulled by a team of four horses. Under the driver's feet was a sack of mail.

"Up ye go, miss," said Simmons, helping Martha into the carriage. A loud cheer broke out from the passengers already inside. Martha's heart leaped with joy at the sight of her brothers.

"Alisdair! Duncan! Robbie!" she cried.

"Where've you been? We've been here half an hour gone!"

"Look, lads, it's the first time in her life she hasna had a word to say!"

The next few minutes were such a confusion of noise and laughter and luggage being tied onto the roof of the carriage that Martha's head was fairly spinning. Almost before she knew what had happened, Simmons had bade her a courteous good-bye and the carriage was rolling down the street on its way out of Perth.

The journey home was quite the opposite of the previous month's trip. Two miles might have passed between one of Father's comments and the next; scarcely two yards passed in silence with Alisdair, Robbie, and Duncan in the carriage. The four Morse children filled the post chaise, so there were no other passengers to frown about noise or fidgeting. Alisdair, who was fifteen now, considered himself responsible for Martha's safety and periodically urged her not to lean too far out of the window; but to Martha's satisfaction, his concerns didn't seem to extend to etiquette. She might wave at shepherds all she liked.

She asked her brothers about school, and

Alisdair obliged with enthusiastic descriptions of his studies. Robbie, sitting beside him, made horrible mocking faces, which vanished in a twinkling whenever Alisdair glanced his way. Martha was hard pressed not to laugh. Duncan took out a little stub of pencil and the crumpled end of his coach ticket, and he sketched faces more horrible still, yet all quite identifiably Robbie's.

Martha felt happiness coming back to her. She was with her brothers; she was going home.

At Crieff they left the post chaise, which was continuing west to Lochearnhead. Father had written Alisdair with instructions to stay overnight in the inn and hire a private carriage to convey them the rest of the way home. Martha shuddered to think of spending another dreadful night with the rats and the bed lumps, but it was not as bad as she feared. The innkeeper put them in a room with two beds—one for Martha, and the other for her brothers to share. The boys' complaints about being squashed and kicked were loud enough to cover any suspiciously ratlike rustlings that might have troubled Martha's sleep.

The carriage was waiting for them after breakfast the next morning. When the driver clucked his tongue to start the horses going, Martha's heart galloped with joy. All the way to Perth, she had strained eagerly for the sight of each new thing; now she was straining to see the familiar. That tree, there—that clump of gorse—surely she had seen them before; surely Auld Mary's hut lay just beyond that rise. . . .

Then there could be no doubt: There was the peat hag, where Father's men cut fuel for the fire; there were Father's sheep, Father's fields of rye. There was the Creag, its stubborn peak jutting proudly above the loch. Thin ghost trails of smoke rose from each of the huts nestled companionably along the shore. A dog ran barking into the path, greeting the carriage, and it was a dog she knew.

They were home. There was only the last little way to go, the short slope up from the loch to the stately gray house on the hill.

Mum came running down the path toward them, catching up her skirts. Martha leaned so far out the carriage window, she was in danger of falling. Alisdair held on to her sash, tugging as if she were a fish he was trying to land.

"You'll crack your head," he scolded.

"Aye, and wind up stone dead like auld MacDougal," teased Robbie.

Martha dropped to her seat.

"That isna funny," she said hotly.

Robbie shrugged unconcernedly, but his eyes showed a glimmer of remorse. Martha glared at him until he turned away, feigning unconcern.

"I'd no idea you were so attached to the auld fellow," he muttered.

"That's because you're a—"

She bit back the harsh words, because she had promised Mum she would try never to wound someone with her tongue. And there was Mum now, opening the door of the carriage, which had rattled to a stop.

Martha threw herself out of the carriage into

her mother's arms, smelling her familiar rose-water scent and feeling the good silk smoothness upon her cheek.

"Martha lass," laughed her mother, holding her tight. The boys crowded around them, all talking at once, and Mum was laughing and kissing their cheeks over Martha's head.

Martha did not think she would ever leave home again.

Glencaraid

There were so many things to say, and so many people to say them to, that the children all but talked themselves hoarse. The boys were always expected to give a full account of their months at school, and Mum wanted to hear all about the journey home. Miss Crow had returned from Loch Katrine the previous week and had a series of funny stories about the cousins with whom she had boarded for her holiday. Mum had messages from all the cousins at Fairlie across the loch.

"And t'other day I met the wee Gow lass on the path, and she made so bold as to ask after you, Martha." Mum smiled. "She bade me pass along her mither's regards."

"Sorcha!" said Martha. She could not wait to see her small friend again.

Cook made a feast of everyone's favorite things. Miss Crow's eyebrows went up at the sight of almond cream, quince pie, roast rabbit, and stewed berries.

"And here's a nice skirl-in-the-pan, lassie," said Cook, spooning a generous helping of the thick, savory porridge onto Martha's plate herself. She would not let the housemaid wait on Martha—Cook, who had not waited at table since she was a maidservant many years ago in the unfathomable past.

It was lovely to be home.

The next morning, Martha slept late. When she woke at last, she had a moment of not knowing where she was. Then she heard Miss Crow humming, and she remembered. Miss Crow was dressed already, tucking the pins into her tidy bun of hair. Shona, the new housemaid, came into the nursery with the breakfast porridge and cream. Thumps and voices murmured through the wall from Grisie's old room, which was now fitted up for the boys. Everything was just right, just as it should be. Even the rain beating against the nursery windows was right, because it was Glencaraid rain.

As soon as she had eaten, dressed, and run across the hall to kiss her mother, Martha went down to the kitchen. She nearly collided with Cook in the doorway, but Cook did not scold.

"Here's herself!" Cook said cheerfully. "Quite the lie-abed this mornin', eh?"

"Lazy Martha, will ye get up?
Will ye get up, will ye get up,"

sang the kitchenmaid, Gertrude, who was washing the breakfast dishes in a pail of water.

"Our wee Martha's a fine city lady noo, the kind what sleeps till noon," teased Cook. "I suppose ye'll expect to be waited on hand and foot now, hmm?"

Martha laughed.

"The servants at Doune House were cross all the time," she said. "At least Kitty was. I scarcely saw the others."

Cook snorted, showing what she thought of city servants.

The talk that day was all of Mr. MacDougal's funeral, which had been held the day before Martha and the boys had returned home. Father had gone, and Uncle Harry and Aunt Grisell from Fairlie. Mum had stayed home to wait for Martha and the boys, uncertain as to the exact date of their arrival.

"Och, I'd like to have been there when they laid the auld laird to rest," said Cook. "I do love a good funeral."

"I heard there were more'n a hundred mourners," said Gertrude wonderingly.

Cook nodded. "And they'll hang on there a fortnight or more, mark my words, eatin' Mrs. MacDougal's larder bare. Aye, there's naught harder on a cook than a family death. I can only hope my time comes long afore there's any deaths in *this* family."

Martha shuddered. She didn't like the thought of Cook's dying any more than the thought of it happening to her own father or mother.

"I wish no one ever had to die," she said passionately.

Cook tousled her hair with a floury hand.

"There's a better world awaitin' us after this one," she said.

"I like this one fine," said Martha.

"Ye'll like that one too, darlin'," Cook said comfortably. "Ye'll see."

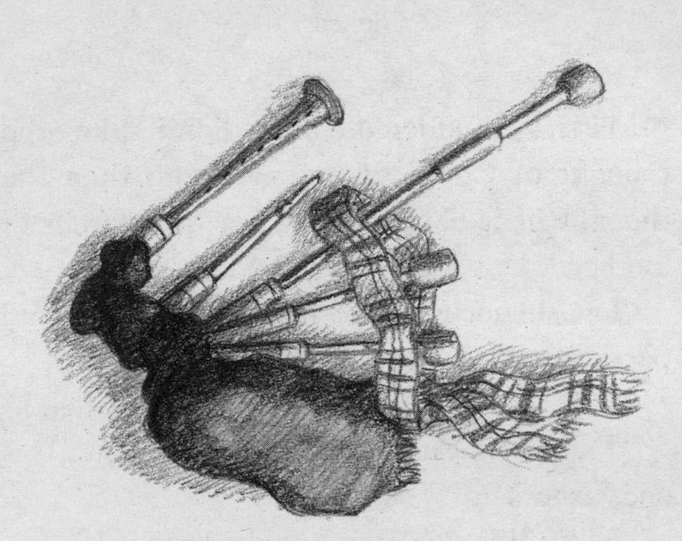

The Ceilidh

"Let's have a ceilidh," said Mum, the following week, "now the children are home."

Word spread quickly from the Stone House to the cottages, and across the loch to the village and beyond. A ceilidh was glad news.

Martha carried the news herself to the cottage beyond the wood, where the Gow family lived.

"There's to be a ceilidh! Everyone's invited," she gasped, breathless from her long run. The moment she was out of sight of the

Stone House, she had tucked up her skirts and stripped off her shoes and stockings. She untucked her skirts now, but she left her shoes with the stockings wadded inside them on the ground outside the cottage. Mrs. Gow tipped her an amused smile, but she said nothing.

"Is it really true?" cried little Sorcha. "A ceilidh at the grand house?"

"Aye," said Martha.

"A ceilidh! A ceilidh!" chanted Ranald.

"Cay-wee!" echoed the Gow baby, clapping his chubby hands.

"Cay-*lee*," corrected Sorcha, who considered it her duty to teach her little brother to speak properly. Try as she might, Mrs. Gow could not convince Sorcha that Peter would learn to speak in his own good time. Sorcha giggled at Peter.

"Look at how glad he is, and he doesn't even know what a grand gatherin' a ceilidh is!"

"Och, Minnie, we *will* go, willna we?" Sorcha begged her mother.

"You must; everyone will!" said Martha firmly.

"Ah, well then, if we must, we must," laughed Mrs. Gow.

"'Tis to be two days hence," Martha told them, "to give Cook a day for the baking."

Cook had no time for stories that day or the next. She bustled and baked all day long, and Gertrude swore she never sat down from dusk to dawn, so busy did Cook keep her. Martha spent half the day in the kitchen, making a batch of currant cakes all on her own. She spent the other half sorting through the presents she had brought back from Perth for her cousins. She had not seen them since her return, and Grisie had sent a number of pretty things for Janet and the others, in addition to the trinkets Martha had purchased with her own pocket money. She was especially pleased with the hair comb she had bought for cousin Meg; it was ornamented with a tiny painted peacock, very like the one on the rug in Meg's room at Fairlie.

The morning of the ceilidh was bright and warm, as if heaven had prepared this day especially for the occasion. Makeshift tables were set up on the grassy hilltop beyond the garden of the Stone House. People came from every corner of Father's land and beyond. Uncle Harry's family ferried over the loch from Fairlie, and all the villagers of Clachan came, and Mum and Father's friends from all over the parish. The kindly old laird of Alroch came cantering along the mountain road on his fine black horse, and Martha rushed to greet him. He was like a grandfather to her, and she had not seen him since she came home from Perth. He reached into his pocket and produced a small cloth sack of sweets. Mum liked to joke that Alroch would bring a bag of sweets for Martha even on her wedding day, so faithfully did he remember her fondness for sugar candy.

"By heaven, lass, how ye've grown!" he declared.

Martha's smile faltered, for she remembered how Mr. MacDougal had said something very similar. It occurred to her that Alroch was as old a man as the laird of Balliecruin had been—older, perhaps.

"What's this? Sure and a cloud has passed

o'er the sun," said old Alroch.

Martha shook her head and made herself smile again. She thanked him for the sweets and began handing them around to the other children. Little Sorcha Gow popped one into her mouth, and her eyes went huge with delight. She had never tasted sugar candy before.

Two or three men with fiddles had begun to play a reel, and Sandy produced his bagpipes. A ring of dancers formed on the most level part of the hill. Martha grabbed Duncan's arm and pulled him toward the dancing. All her old chums were there: Una Shaw, Annie Davis, Lew Tucker, Ian Cameron. Nannie Cameron, who had once been Cook's kitchen-maid, stood beside the fiddlers, bouncing her baby back and forth in time. The baby laughed and laughed.

Up the hill an old man came tramping, a tall staff in his hand and his long gray hair blowing back behind him from under his Highland bonnet. He wore a faded red plaid kilted around his waist and slung over his shoulder in the old way. His bare knees showed above threadbare stockings.

"The storyteller!" cried one of the children, and the cry was picked up by the rest.

"The storyteller! 'Tis auld Giles Kippletringan!"

Father had sent for Giles Kippletringan especially, of course. He was a seanachie, a wandering tale-teller, and it would not have been a proper ceilidh without him. It was said he was the only man in Perthshire who was a match for Auld Mary at holding an audience breathless.

The old man lifted a hand in greeting, his eyes crinkled into squinting crescents. His face was seamed and weathered, and his boots were brown with dust. It was said he had walked as many miles in his lifetime as if he'd been to London and back a hundred times; and yet he had never left the parish in which he was born. He walked from village to village, telling his stories and taking his meals wherever they were offered.

Father greeted him cordially.

"Welcome, seanachie. Will ye give us a tale?"

"Ah, well then," said Giles Kippletringan slowly, scratching his ear and feigning reluctance, "if it's insistin', ye are, sir, what choice have I?"

Father smiled, and a cheer went up from the crowd.

"A tale, a tale!"

He rose from his bench, and a hush fell.

"I suppose," said Giles Kippletringan, "I might tell ye aboot the time the lass outtalked the kelpie . . ."

"Aye!" called the crowd, stamping and cheering.

"Now dinna ye be thinkin' I'm meanin' our Miss Martha," said Giles Kippletringan, winking broadly, "though I dinna doubt fer a moment she could do it her own self."

Laughter swept over the crowd, and Duncan elbowed Martha in the ribs. Everywhere people turned to grin at her. She laughed too, feeling rather honored that he had singled her out.

"Well then," said Giles Kippletringan, "here's how it happened."

The Seanachie's Story

A lass there was once, daughter of a weaver. A bonny, blithe thing was she, with a merry heart and a quick step. Every day, morn and evenin', she went out to fetch her mither a pail o' water from the well beyond the way; and that's how the trouble came upon her.

'Twas near the end o' her sixteenth summer she went out in the gloamin' wi' her pail in her hand, and she came back trippin' as light as ivver. But when her mither asked her if she'd met anyone in the wood, the lass opened her mouth to say, "Nary a soul," and all that came out was silence. And though she tried and tried, not a word could she utter.

"She's been cursed," said her mither; but the lass couldna say how it had come aboot. Not even in her own thoughts, for she kenned not why the misfortune had fallen upon her. Days passed, and weeks passed, and not a word passed her lips.

Her father and her mither were sore grieved, for they missed their lass's sweet voice singin' over her spinnin' wheel of an evenin', and her merry laugh ripplin' through the hoose as she went aboot her work in the day. Mither and father went aboot with long faces and heavy hearts. The hoose grew altogether silent, for their daughter's misfortune seemed to have stilled their own tongues.

How long this might ha' gone on I canna say. But one evenin' when the rain fell heavy and the wind was high, there came a knock at the door. The lass hurried to open it, wonderin' who might be so unlucky as to be out in such a gale. The rain beat in through the open door, wettin' the lass to the skin, and a great gust o' wind seemed to blow a wee auld woman right into the kitchen.

"Lord ha' mercy!" the lass's mither cried.

"Quick, shut the door afore we're all washed away!" cried the lass's father.

The lass closed the door against the wind and the rain, and they all stood a moment gawpin' at the wee auld woman.

Wet as a herring, she was, wi' the rainwater drippin' off her garments and aye runnin' right off the tip o' her nose. The lass snatched her own shawl from off her shoulders and gave it to the wee auld woman to dry herself wi', and the lass's mither fetched some dry clothes. In no time at all the auld woman was toasting herself by the fire, admirin' the fine weave o' the frock the goodwife had given her to wear. She thanked them for their kindness and declared she'd nivver in her life seen any sight so welcome as the light o' their candles shining in the window through the cauld rain.

"I've come a fair piece, and I've a fair piece to go," she said, and told them how she was on her way to her great-grandchild's christenin' at Fowlis Wester. "'Tis a hard walk for auld bones, but where there's a will, there's a way, says I."

Noo it wasna long afore t'auld woman noticed the lass's silence, and she asked the weaver's wife what was amiss wi' her daughter. The goodwife explained the sad mystery. T'auld woman nodded and looked wise.

"Och, aye," she croaked. "She was after fetchin' water from the well, ye say. Tell me, lass, after ye left the well that evenin', did ye miss a ring or a necklace, or happen a hairpin or some such?"

The lass's eyes went wide, and she nodded aye. She touched the comb in her bonny brown hair to show that 'twas a comb she'd lost the day of her misfortune.

"Ah, ye see there," said t'auld woman. "I can tell ye just what happened to yer comb. Fell in the water, it did, as ye were leanin' o'er the well. I'll warrant there's a kelpie taken o'er that well, and ye've made him mortal angry. He'll have nae peace in that well so long as yer pretty comb lies in it. Cursed ye, he has, in revenge."

Well, 'twas a great relief to the lass and her parents, kennin' the reason for her misfortune. 'Twas a greater relief to ken that what had been done could be undone, for 'twas a simple matter to go and fetch the comb oot o' the well. The weaver and his wife thanked t'auld woman over and over, and the lass kissed her wrinkled hand to show how grateful she was.

The next mornin' was a fine sunny mornin', and t'auld woman said she'd be on her way. The weaver wouldna hear o' her makin' the rest o' her journey afoot, and sure he harnessed his own mare to his wagon and drove her to Fowlis Wester himself. And 'twas a good thing, too, as he found oot later.

The lass, just as soon as she'd finished wipin' the dishes for her mither, hurried oot to the kelpie's well and fetched her lost comb frae oot o' the water. She hurried home, half afraid to try and see if the curse had been lifted. Her mither met her at the door, tremblin' wi' hope.

"Well?" she asked, and the lass answered her, "I—I dinna ken!"

Then she laughed in delight, for she *did* ken noo. The curse had been lifted.

Or so they thought. The lass had been silent for sae long, her mither could not get enough o' her sweet, liltin' voice. She listened wi' a glad heart as the lass chattered away all the forenoon. Aroond aboot dinnertime, the weaver came home, and his heart fair split wi' joy when he heard his daughter singin' in the kitchen.

But the sun had not set that night afore the weaver and his wife had a new worry. Their lass had scarcely stopped talkin' long enough to draw breath all that day. Not fer all the gold in Christendom would they ha' gone back to the way she'd been that mornin', mute as the grave; but sure they couldna help be a mite worrited that somethin' had gone amiss. Would the lass nivver stop chatterin' for a moment?

It seemed she would not. She talked in her sleep, and she talked when she woke, and not once the next day did she ivver cease talkin'. Nor the next, nor the next. The nights were the worst, for her prattlin' and singin' and laughin' made it quite impossible for the man and his wife to get a wink o' sleep.

After the third sleepless night, the weaver and his wife bethought themselves o' the wise auld woman who'd helped them afore. The weaver harnessed his mare and rode directly to Fowlis Wester, thankin' the Almighty he kenned just where to go to fetch t'auld woman. The wee auld woman was delighted to see him, and she listened with great interest to the news o' his daughter.

"Go home and ask yer lass if she dried

the comb well afore she put it in her hair," she said, when he'd finished. "If but one drop o' water remained on the comb, she'll have angered the kelpie all o'er again. And if that's the case, then I'll tell ye what she must do to break the curse."

The weaver listened wi' all his might. He hurried home and asked the lass if she'd dried the comb well afore puttin' it in her hair. The lass clapped a hand to her mouth in horror. "Och, dearie me, father," she said. "I nivver thought to dry it at all. I was that glad to have it back and break the curse, I just stuck it in me hair drippin' wet. Och, what've I done? I've gone and made the curse worse than ivver, for who'll stand to be around me if I canna stop blatherin' for two seconds together? How will I ivver go to kirk again, or—"

'Twas wi' some difficulty her father interrupted her. "Dinna fret, lass. Here's what ye must do. Go straight back to the well and talk to the kelpie. T'auld woman told me if ye can outtalk him, 'twill break the spell. Just ye bide there and talk until he gives up, mind."

The lass beamed at him. "Och, aye, Father, I will! I'll nivver quit until he frees me from the curse, I promise ye that. I'll talk and talk and talk and talk and talk—"

"Whisht!" cried her mither. "Go on then!"

And so the lass went. She hied her to the well and she leaned o'er it, and she called oot to the kelpie.

"Good mornin'!" cried she.

"Good mornin'," mocked the kelpie.

"I've come to talk to you," she said politely.

"Talk to you," he mocked in return.

She knelt there all the mornin', and all the afternoon, chatterin' away to him for all she was worth. Sure, and she was rather enjoyin' herself. She told every story she kenned, and she sang every song she'd ever

learned, and she recited all the hymns from the psalter. But always the kelpie had a mockin' reply.

Night was comin' on fast, and still the lass leaned o'er the well, though her back was stiff and sore, and she was beginnin' to tremble a bit at the thought o' keepin' by the well through the dark o' night. To make matters worse, a cauld rain began to fall. But the lass had promised her parents she would stay at the well until the curse was lifted, and she was determined to keep her promise.

"I'll talk the night through," she told the kelpie.

"The night through," agreed the kelpie, and the lass's heart quailed within her.

But just as the rain began to pour down in earnest, the lass's parents came hurryin' through the trees toward the well. They'd spent the long, anxious day frettin' aboot their poor daughter and aye beginnin' to fear for her safety. Wi' the dark night fallin', they decided they cared not whether she talked too much or too little, so long as she was safe and hale. So they'd hurried to the well to tell her so. Their hearts ached at the sight o' their poor lass hunched o'er the well, so weary and cauld. They called oot to her to nivver mind the kelpie and come on home.

The lass sighed a great happy sigh.

"Ah, kelpie," she said. "Sure and I've enjoyed talkin' to ye. I was of a mind to go on talkin' all the night through."

"All the night through?" asked the kelpie, his voice soundin' as weary as the lass felt.

"Aye," she answered, "and tomorrow as well. But alas, me mither and father have come to tell me 'tis time for me to leave now."

The kelpie's voice came roaring out of the well.

"Leave now!"

And so the lass rose and went gladly to her parents. The three of them went home together with thankful hearts, and from that day on, the lass talked neither too much nor too little. But nivver again did she go out in the gloamin' to fetch water from the kelpie's well.

Afterward, there was piping and dancing until long after the sun sank behind the green mountains. Martha ate until her belly ached, and she sang herself hoarse, and she danced until she was so dizzy that the mountains wheeled around her in a ring dance of their own, while the bagpipes crooned.

The Quiet House

The rest of the boys' holidays passed in a rush of noise and fun. Suddenly they were over, and the boys returned to Perth. Without them, the Stone House seemed shocked into a silence as hushed as Doune House had been after Mr. MacDougal's death. Martha half expected to see sheets draped over the looking glasses.

At dinner the first day, Martha stared at the empty places and felt her heart shrink within her. She had never realized before how awful it was to be the youngest. None of her siblings had had to stay behind while the others went out into the world. They had all had each other during their growing-up time. She could remember when they had played together on the Creag, or rowed in Robbie's little boat to the brushy island on the far side of Loch Caraid, where they had fashioned a little playhouse among the willows. They had made a ring of stones for a fireplace and had roasted potatoes in the ashes. They had painted their faces with blackberry juice to look like war markings for fierce games of chiefs at war.

Now they were all growing up. The old times seemed so far away that they might as well have belonged to someone else, like the adventures in Mum's stories.

"What is it, lass? You've had scarcely a bite," asked Mum. "Are you ill?"

Martha shook her head and said she was all right. She did not know how to say anything more. You could not say you were sorry that people had to grow up.

A restless something reared up inside her,

a queer sort of ache that disturbed her all the more because she thought she had left her aching behind at Doune House. She was home; home was lovely. She ought to be happy. There were no long, idle, lonely hours of yearning for someone to talk to. She had plenty of people to talk to—Mum, and Cook, and Miss Crow, and all her old friends on the estate. But she missed Grisie, missed their talks. She missed her brothers—Duncan especially. He talked with his hands, his quick drawings. Martha found herself looking at people and wondering how Duncan would capture their expressions.

She was quieter than she used to be, because she did not know how to speak of the things that were stirring in her heart. Mum regarded her with soft, watchful eyes, and Cook asked if she was feeling quite herself. Even Father noticed, asking whether she had lost her tongue in Perth. Martha felt a wave of pleasure at this, for she had thought he did not notice anything about her. But Father seemed to approve of the change, and that made the ache fiercer. She wanted him to want her back as she had always been, before she went away.

She was not always thinking troublesome thoughts, for her days were full. In the mornings, there were lessons with Miss Crow, and in the afternoons, Mum was teaching her to spin on the flax wheel. She was old enough now. She remembered when she had been too small to work the treadle. How difficult it had seemed then! It was not so very hard. Her fingers knew their work already, for it was very much like using the drop spindle. Easier, because her feet did part of the work. Her foot pumped the treadle, the wheel turned round, and her fingers shaped the combed flax fibers into a narrow thread.

Flax must be wet spun to make the thread smooth, so she was constantly dipping her fingers into a little cup of water that fit into a shelf on the spinning wheel. It was tedious work, but it left her mind free to listen to Mum. Mum had always told stories to the children while she spun. Now there was only

Martha left at home, and Mum's stories were different. She told Martha of the old days, when her grandfather had been a Drummond clansman. She told her of growing up on Skye, in her auntie's home, where the villagers gathered seaweed to burn in their hearths and the selkies were said to shed their sealskins on moonlight nights and dance on human legs along the barren shores.

"Did you nivver see one?" asked Martha, breathless with wonder.

Mum chuckled. "Och, nay, nivver. Though not for want o' trying. I used to creep to me window in the night and peer out at the shore, hoping at least for a glimpse o' an empty sealskin folded up neat on the rocks. If I'd seen one, I was bound and determined to slip out o' the house and snatch it up, and then when a wee selkie lass came searching for it, I'd make friends wi' her, and she'd teach me to swim beneath the waves as she did. Och, how I did strain me eyes staring through the dark, studying that shore!"

"Canna we go someday?" Martha pleaded.

"I want to see it myself!"

"Alas, the auld house is no more," said Mum sorrowfully. "Caught fire, it did, long years ago, and burned to the ground. My auntie passed the rest o' her days with her daughter, my cousin Anne, in Ayrshire."

She smiled at the disappointed look in Martha's eyes and said that perhaps someday they would go to Skye to see where the old house had stood. Martha's heart leaped at the thought. She had been to the eastern edge of Scotland now, where the Tay rolled into the sea; she longed to see the western shores, with their green craggy islands and the foamy waves beating against the cliffs.

Dead Martha

Michaelmas came. Father's tenants paid their quarterly rents, and since they most often paid in rabbits and hens, cabbages and pigeons, every meal for weeks held some surprise or other. Martha was glad of the hearty meals, for the strong winds of autumn stirred her appetite. She worked hard at her lessons in the mornings, and she played on the moor in the afternoons.

October passed, and All Hallow's Eve came, with its bonfires and games. All the children of Glencaraid came knocking on the door of the Stone House that night, singing songs and delightedly pocketing the pennies Father distributed. Then came November, with its short, gray days and increasingly chilly nights. One November night, Martha's stomach began to ache. The bedcovers were smothering; she kicked at them, but they grabbed at her legs. Miss Crow made complaining noises in her sleep and jerked the covers back up over her own shoulders. Martha came suddenly out of her half sleep and knew she was going to be sick. There was nothing nearby but the chamber pot. It was full. She could not use that. Moaning with frustration, she stumbled across the room toward the washbasin. She reached it just in time.

She had never been so miserable in her life. She hunched over the basin, retching, and it seemed as if she would fly into pieces. Her head throbbed. The floor was cold as Loch Caraid. Martha was shivering, shivering, and she could not stop.

Then Miss Crow's hands were smoothing back her hair, holding it away from the basin. Martha had not heard her get up. The governess wrapped something soft and warm around Martha's shoulders, and her gentle voice murmured soothing words.

"Poor lass, you'll be all right. Have you finished?"

Martha nodded weakly. She did not see how there could be anything left to come up. Miss Crow brought her some water to rinse her mouth. She helped Martha back into bed.

"There, child. Sleep."

The bed was so warm, she began to cry. Slowly she stopped shivering. Miss Crow sat beside her, stroking her hair until she fell asleep.

Martha was sick all the next day. Mum sat beside her, sewing, while she slept; or else Miss Crow was there, knitting quietly, her face lively with her private thoughts. Martha liked to watch Miss Crow think. You could see the ideas move across her brow, and her mouth quirked slightly as if in amusement or quiet delight.

When Miss Crow looked up and caught Martha watching her, she smiled crookedly with her eyebrows raised, as if to say she pitied anyone who had nothing better to do than to watch her knit. She set the knitting aside and took up her little leather-covered psalter and read to Martha, while the orange afternoon sun slanted beneath the drawn curtains and crept across the nursery floor.

Praise the Lord from the earth, ye dragons,
and all deeps:
Fire, and hail; snow, and vapour;
stormy wind fulfilling his word.

In the afternoon, there came a tap on the nursery door, and Shona entered, followed by Auld Mary. The wise old healer woman laid her wrinkled hand upon Martha's forehead.

"We'll have ye back on yer pretty wee feet in nae time," she said cheerfully, and she went to the hearth with her satchel of herbs and brewed Martha a tea of willowbark and tansy. It was bitter and hot, but Martha worried it down. She thought it would make her feel better right away, but it did not. She was still miserably sick to her stomach. But she did not ache and shiver and burn for a long while, after that tea.

Mum gave her more tea that evening, and Martha slept deeply for a time. But she woke in the night tossing and kicking at the sheets, and had another bout of huddling over a basin while Mum smoothed back her hair. She slept a long time the next morning, waking to hear Mum and Miss Crow talking in hushed tones before the nursery hearth.

"*You* go, Lydia; I shall stay home with Martha," Mum was saying.

"You are very kind, Mrs. Morse, but I do not mind staying behind."

Martha realized wonderingly that they meant going to kirk. She felt amazed that Sunday had come already. She could only faintly remember Friday, and Saturday was like a dream that had already faded before she woke.

"No," said Mum. "I'll hear no more about it. I quite insist. You go now, before the ferryman leaves without you."

Martha felt cross and tired. Her head ached, and she did not like to hear them arguing.

"Why dinna you both go?" she said, rather irritably.

Mum gave a start, and both heads turned toward the bed.

"So you're awake, are you?" Swiftly Mum came to the bedside to smile down at Martha.

"I dinna like it when you argue," said Martha stubbornly.

"Why, darling! We werena arguing! We were merely discussing which o' us shall stay home from kirk to keep you company."

Martha frowned, feeling hot inside and out. They did not want to leave her alone. It gave her the queerest creeping feeling, as if something unpleasant were crawling up her spine. She thought of Mr. MacDougal, lying immobile in his bed. Kitty had panicked over leaving him even for a minute, lest he die all alone.

Martha huddled under the quilt, her stomach roiling.

"All right," said Miss Crow, "I will go, if you insist, Mrs. Morse. But do let me sit with Martha long enough for you to have a little breakfast. The ferry will not leave so soon as all that."

"I assure you it is not necessary, Lydia—"

Martha could bear it no longer. The words exploded out of her.

"Dinna be so daft! You can leave me alone; I'm not about to die!"

"Martha!" cried Mum in shock. Martha heard Miss Crow's surprised intake of breath. For a long moment no one spoke, and then:

"I see," murmured the governess.

A little choked sound escaped her mother.

"Och, my lass," murmured Mum. "Is that what you've been thinking?"

"Isna it?" said Martha weakly.

"Not a bit o' it!" cried Mum. "Do you not

think I'd send for a doctor, if I feared for a moment you were in serious danger?"

Martha had not thought of that.

"You sent for Auld Mary. She's better than a doctor."

"I sent for her because I kenned she could ease your suffering, that's all. Did not her tea make you feel better?"

"Mm-hmm."

"You're a strong, hearty lass," said Miss Crow briskly. "You've no reason to fear."

"Cora MacDougal was strong and hearty too," said Martha. "Everyone at Doune House said so."

"Cora Mac—" Mum's eyes widened with understanding. "You speak truly. I mind the day we heard the news o' the MacDougals' sad loss. 'Twas a terrible, tragic thing, Martha, I'll not deny it. But that was an entirely different case. You've had no tainted fish. 'Tis a passing illness, and you'll be right as rain in a few more days. Why, you're a great deal better already. You've enough strength to be naughty, have you not?"

Martha couldn't help but smile at that. Miss Crow kissed her and went to put on her Sunday dress, and that morning Mum made a little kirk of the nursery, singing hymns as Martha sipped Auld Mary's bitter, soothing tea.

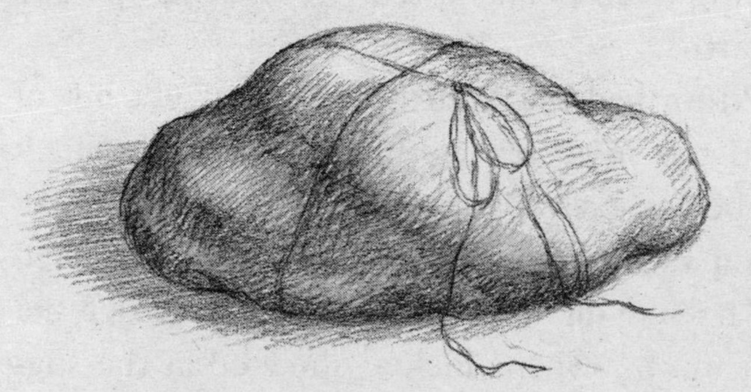

Fairy Dolls

The next morning Martha was feeling much better, but now Miss Crow was sick. Mum insisted that the governess move to Grisie's old room, next door to the nursery, so she might be assured of quiet and rest. Then Mum fell ill, and then Father. The sickness was making its way through the house. Auld Mary came every day with herb teas and tonics. Cook boiled beef to make a weak broth for the invalids. The maids were kept busy scuttling chamber pots and basins outdoors to be emptied on the rubbish heap, and changing bed linens, and laying fresh peats on the fires in the upstairs hearths.

Mum had said Martha must not get out of bed too soon. It was maddening to be stuck in bed when your stomach felt perfectly fine, even rather hungry, and your muscles ached to be moving. She begged Shona to let her get up, but Shona looked shocked at the suggestion.

"Against yer mither's wishes? Rake me o'er the coals, she would, if I dared!"

"But I'm quite well! If you'll just let me run and ask her . . ."

Shona's eyes went wide with alarm. She entreated Martha to do no such thing. Mum was too ill to be disturbed, she said, and then she closed her mouth abruptly and left the room. Martha had nothing to do but lie there, and now she was worried about Mum. Perhaps her mother was more ill than she herself had been; perhaps she was not as hearty as Martha. Perhaps—

Martha groaned aloud out of worry and

frustration. She heard quick steps in the passage, and Shona burst back into the room clutching a basin, saying, "Are ye well, miss?"

Martha bit her lip, ashamed at having made Shona worry.

"Aye, I'm well," she muttered guiltily.

Shona looked cross.

"Ye must no fret, Miss Martha, but do yer duty cheerfully," she said impatiently. "As yer dear mither expects ye to. Dinna go makin' mair work for us as is runnin' our poor feet off already."

Martha was very sorry, and she begged Shona to forgive her.

"Whisht, dinna worrit yerself into a frenzy. Ye're a good lass."

It struck Martha that Shona looked none too well herself. Now that she thought of it, she could recall hearing coughing from above her in the attic, where Shona and Gertrude slept. She had not thought what would happen if the servants became ill. Who would take care of them?

She wished Grisie were here. She and

Kenneth lived close enough now to visit; Martha could not understand why they did not come.

"Shona? Canna we send for me sister?"

But Shona shook her head and said young Mrs. MacDougal must not risk taking ill herself.

"Kenneth, then," Martha suggested, thinking that he would at least bring some mirth to the quiet house.

Shona snorted. "To nurse ye? What kens he of tendin' the sick? I mean nae disrespect," she added, "for I ken he's a fine man and a good master to his tenants and servants. They're all glad at Balliecruin that he's in charge noo, they are. But tendin' sickbed is best left to them as has some experience o' it."

"He has experience. Didna he sit wi' his father for ivver so many days?"

But Shona had bustled out without answering. Miss Crow was calling weakly from Grisie's old room. Martha listened from her bed to Shona's voice murmuring soothingly, and Miss Crow coughing. She heard Father coughing down the hall. She heard Cook coughing in the kitchen below. Restless and miserable, she lay there waiting for Shona to come again. She sang to amuse herself:

"The Laird o' Cockpen, he's proud and he's great,
His mind is ta'en up wi' things o' the State . . ."

And:

"John Anderson, my jo, John,
When we were first acquent,
Your locks were like the raven,
Your bonny brow was brent;
But now your brow is beld, John;
Your locks are like the snow;
But blessing on your frosty pow,
John Anderson, my jo!"

Perhaps she my-joed too enthusiastically,

for Shona came once more hurrying into the nursery.

"Miss Martha, ye must keep quiet! Yer mither's finally restin' a bit, poor lady. Here, let me bring ye yer wee dollies."

She snatched the box containing Martha's fairy dolls off the chest of drawers and all but dumped it in Martha's lap. Then she hurried out again, leaving Martha staring.

It had been months since she'd thought about her fairy dolls. She much preferred playing outside to sitting alone in her room with toys. But her heart gave a little stab of tenderness when she opened the wooden case and saw the dear fairy baby in its walnut-shell cradle, and its dainty mother and grinning father. Auld Mary had made these dolls long ago, and Duncan had given them to Martha as a present.

Martha remembered the day he had brought them home. It had been Hogmanay, New Year's Eve, the winter before Alisdair and Robbie had first gone away to school. That was the last year all of them had lived at home together. She had never guessed, then, that things would one day be different.

She felt very old. In another month, she would be eleven, and that really was getting to be rather grown up. Of course, she was too old now to play with dolls, but as she sat there turning her fairy dolls over in her hands, she felt the same glad affection for them that she had had when she was little. She admired their wee clothes, made from scraps of felted wool, and their cunning wooden faces with the ears carved into little points. Auld Mary was a clever hand at doll making.

Martha thought she would like to try to make some fairy dolls herself. She could give them to Sorcha and the other children on Father's estate. That was something she could do right there in her bed, if she only had the materials. She thought about calling Shona and asking her to fetch things, but she remembered the housemaid's tired eyes and anxious brow.

Cook's voice from below caught her attention, for the kitchen was directly beneath Martha's room. She could hear Cook greeting someone who had just come in. Perhaps it was Auld Mary, come to visit the patients. That would be perfect; Martha was certain Auld Mary would be pleased to get her just what she needed for the dolls.

Martha threw herself flat on her stomach and hung her head off the bed, looking for a hole in the floor. All the floorboards had small holes at one end that had been drilled at the lumberyard in Lochearnhead so that the boards might be tied together for their wagon journey north. Many a time Martha and her brothers had spied on Cook through the holes, trying to see what she was serving for dinner.

She had to slide halfway to the floor in order to see through the hole, but her legs were still on the bed, so no one could say she was disobeying her mother's instructions. She put her eye to the hole and peered through. Cook was talking to someone—a boy. Martha could see the top of his cap. Cook moved toward the pantry, evidently fetching something for the lad, and he stood quietly waiting. His cap was smeared with soot. Martha knew who it was: Lew Tucker, the blacksmith's son.

"Lew!" she whispered, putting her mouth to the hole. "Lew Tucker! Up here!"

"Eh?" said Lew, looking upward. He broke into a curious grin. "Miss Martha, is it?"

"Stay right there—I shall drop something down!" she called. "Half a minute."

She inched herself backward onto the bed and scooted around to lean off the other side, toward the table at which she sat to do her lessons. She could just barely reach it. Her fingertips brushed the edge of her copybook; that was what she was after. She held tight to the bedpost and leaned a bit farther—there! She had it. Then, in a rather more precarious maneuver, she managed to take hold of her quill pen and use it to slide the ink bottle along the table until she could grasp it.

Quickly she scrawled, managing to spill no more than half a dozen drops of ink upon the covers:

Dear Lew please help, I am much obliged. I am not allowed out of bed. Can you get me some bits of felt or cloth, any color, also some wood to carve and a knife. And needle and thread, Cook will give them to you for me. Something for doll hair if you can.

Gratefully yours, Martha Morse.

She blew on the paper to dry the ink and tore the page from her copybook, hoping Miss Crow would not be cross when she discovered it. Rolling the scrap of paper into a tight cylinder, Martha leaned out over the hole in the floor once more. Lew was still below, looking up.

Martha pushed the paper through the hole. It landed at Lew's feet; he knelt to pick it up and pocketed it just as Martha heard Cook come back into the kitchen.

"Here we are," said Cook, but Martha could not see her to tell what she had gone to fetch. Lew grinned up at Martha once more and moved away in the direction of Cook's voice.

Martha heard them talking a little longer, and then there was the sound of a door closing, and silence below. Lew must have gone. Now there was nothing to do but wait. She had no doubt that he would do as she had asked. Lew Tucker was the sort of boy who would walk through a tempest to help out a friend.

Scarcely three quarters of an hour later, Martha heard heavy steps coming up the stairs. Cook entered her room, red-faced, one hand on her broad hip and the other holding out a small cloth-wrapped bundle.

"Here's some odd doin's," she declared. "Young Lew Tucker was here not an hour gone, fetchin' a cheese yer father promised in trade for a bit o' ironwork. Noo he comes marchin' back, he does, as polite as ye please, askin' if I wouldna mind deliverin' a parcel to Miss Martha—her bein' bedridden an' all."

She placed the bundle on the bed and stood looking on with upraised eyebrows, clearly intending to wait there while Martha opened it. Martha grinned at her and eagerly pulled off the string that held the parcel closed. The cloth fell open, revealing a tumble of objects.

"What in the world?" asked Cook.

"It's for making dolls," Martha explained, exploring the pile. Lew had found everything she'd asked for, and more. There were some scraps of black and yellow felt, a large piece of red wool, a coil of thick brown yarn, four or five stout twigs, a stub of pencil, a needle and thread, and a battered pocketknife.

"Why, the lad's gone and given ye his very own knife," cried Cook. "Martha, what sort o' mischief have ye been at? Ye're no supposed to stir from yer bed."

"I didna! I gave Lew a message when he was here before. Me feet never touched the floor, I promise!"

"Um-hmm," said Cook, looking suspicious. She pointed at a slip of paper among the scraps of cloth. "Sent ye a message, he has."

Martha snatched it up, excited. Lew's handwriting was neater than hers, but his spelling was rather worse.

Dear Miss Martha,

I am glad to help. I askd Missus Sandy at the cottiges if I coud go throug her rag bag. She was glad to help to. The cloth and thred and needle are from her. Pleese keep the nife with my complyments. I ken youll make fine dolls. If I can do anything else for ye just ask. I hope your hale again soon and the rest o your house is to.

Your frend,
Lewis Tucker

Cook was reading over Martha's shoulder, her bosom shaking with silent laughter.

"Och, the twa o' ye are quite a pair. I dinna doubt that lad'd go to the ends o' the earth if ye but asked him. Well, ye've plenty to keep busy wi' now, and no mistakin'. Now happen poor Shona can get a spot o' rest!"

As Old as the Year

When at last the sickness had crept back out of the Stone House, rather more slowly than it had come in, winter had arrived in earnest. The loch was frozen, the fields bleak and still. Mum instructed the maids to build the fires high, and even Father stayed indoors most of the time. He liked to hear Martha play the pianoforte, and hardly a day passed when he did not urge her to "give us a tune." He was quite pleased with how much she had improved since her visit to Perth.

"We'll make a lady o' ye yet," he said, "me bonny wild lass."

There was the fun of Hogmanay. This year, the Hogmanay festivities were held at Uncle Harry's house, across the loch. It was a lively family reunion, for Kenneth and Grisie came by carriage from Balliecruin. And then, the very next day, Martha celebrated her eleventh birthday. Cook said it was lucky to have a birthday on the first day of the year. Indeed, Martha thought it felt grand, becoming a year older at the same time the world did. Mum gave her a bead necklace, and Father gave her some sheet music for the pianoforte. Grisie gave her an exquisitely embroidered cushion for her room. But Miss Crow's gift was Martha's favorite: a slim leather-bound edition of Shakespeare's sonnets, all for her own.

"I'll learn them all by heart," Martha declared.

Miss Crow smiled. "I've no doubt that you will. Of course then I suppose you'll have little use for the book, will you?"

"I'll love it anyway," said Martha. "And if I have a daughter someday, I'll give it to her. And you can live with us and be her governess."

"Oh, heavens," laughed Miss Crow. "I shall be quite ancient by then."

"Och, not *so* old. Younger than Auld Mary, I expect."

Miss Crow's laughter pealed out. "Yes, a bit younger than that."

In March, Father arranged for Mr. Tucker, the blacksmith, to come to Glencaraid to shoe the horses. Lew came also, to help his father. Martha, who loved to hear the glowing iron hiss when it was plunged into a bucket of water, hovered as near to the makeshift forge as she was allowed to get. To her annoyance, this was not terribly near.

She tried to give Lew back his knife, but he wouldn't take it.

"It's yers, miss," he said good-naturedly. "Might come in handy someday. Ye canna tell."

"But you're a boy—you need a knife!" Martha had protested.

Lew had shrugged. "All the same, 'tis yers." His blue eyes shone out at her from his smudged and sooty face.

Martha regarded him steadily, wishing she could think of something to give him in return. She had already given away three of her little handmade fairy dolls: one to Sorcha Gow, one to Nannie's little daughter, Joan, and one to Mrs. Sandy for her small girls. There was one doll left, but of course Lewis would have no use for it.

She ran to the house and fetched it anyway. "Here," she said, thrusting it toward him. "For your wee sister. I want her to have it."

Lew broke into a delighted grin. He cupped the fairy doll gently in his palm, as if it were an egg he feared he might break. He gave a low appreciative whistle.

"Why, Miss Martha, sure and I've nivver seen a bonnier dolly. How'd ye do it? Them stitches is like wee bits o' nothin'!"

"Pooh—my sister Grisie can sew much better than that. Look how crooked my seams are."

Lew shook his head. "I think they be fine,

miss. Thank'ee kindly. Our Elsie'll be that tickled, she'll not ken what to say."

Martha laughed. Little Elsie Tucker was scarcely a year old. She did not know what to say about *anything* yet.

Live Cora

In early April, when the cold gray rains fell every day, Mum packed for a visit to Balliecruin.

"I'll go ahead o' you, Martha," she said. "You and Father shall follow in a few weeks' time."

At first Martha was dismayed to be left behind, but Miss Crow made them merry weeks. She turned the nursery into a theater, hanging a sheet across the middle of the room for a stage curtain. She and Martha rehearsed a selection of scenes from *Romeo and Juliet*, which they performed for the wildly appreciative audience of Father, Cook, Sandy, and the maids. Sandy stomped and cheered when Martha, a brave Romeo, slew the tempestous Tybalt, played with fiery-eyed passion by Miss Crow. Juliet's death scene, which Martha punctuated with a great many jerks and thrashings as the poison seeped through her veins, rendered Cook so weepy that Father had to give her his handkerchief.

"Och, the poor lass," she sobbed. "I canna bear to see her die."

"Indeed," said Father wryly. "I think it's the most painful sight I've ivver seen."

"Truly?" cried Martha, leaping up from her early grave.

"Truly," laughed Father. "Congratulations, Juliet, on an admirable death—and a miraculous recovery."

Between rehearsing the play, watching Father's men give the sheep their spring shearing, and making frequent visits to the stables, where Father's black mare had given birth to a fine, velvet-nosed colt, three weeks flew quickly by. In the fourth week, a rider came from Balliecruin with a message for Father.

Father snatched the letter out of his hand and tore it open.

"A daughter!" he shouted, his face alight with joy. "Both are well; we shall go at once."

"Both *who* are well?" demanded Martha, utterly at a loss to understand why Father was so excited and Miss Crow was clapping her hands with delight.

Father picked Martha up and whirled her around in his strong arms, as he had done when she was a little girl.

"Ye're an auntie," he told her.

"A *what*?"

"Your sister," said Father, "has become a mother. A fine wee lass was born to her yesterday noon. I'm a grandfather, I am!"

Martha stood openmouthed with astonishment.

"A bairn," she said weakly. "Grisie has a bairn."

"Your niece." Miss Crow smiled.

Now it was Martha's turn to clap and whirl.

"A bairn!" she cried. "I'm an auntie!"

Now that she knew, she could not believe she hadn't guessed earlier. She thought with some indignation that Grisie might have told her. Martha could almost hear Mum saying it wasn't proper to talk about such things—*such things*! Why, this was a new person in the family! How could her arrival have been kept a secret?

But looking back, Martha saw that it needn't have been a secret at all. She had missed the signs.

They packed hurriedly—indeed, their packed bags were produced so swiftly that Martha thought the fairies must have conjured them up. Miss Crow had been prepared, waiting for the summons from Balliecruin.

Almost before Martha knew what was happening, she found herself in Father's carriage watching the wet green hills bump past the window. Sim was driving, just as on the journey to Perth. But this time Martha and Father were not alone; Miss Crow sat beside Martha, rapidly knitting a soft woollen bootie so tiny, Martha thought it would fit a brownie's foot.

She could not imagine a baby so small that its foot would fit that bootie. She had seen newborn bairns before, of course, but Mum always said you could never remember how small a new babe was until you held one.

Martha was wild to know what they would name the bairn.

"Will they call her Margaret, after Mum, d'you think?" she asked Miss Crow. Secretly Martha was hoping Grisie would name the baby after her, but of course she could not admit that out loud. She added, trying to sound nonchalant, "Or—what's Mrs. MacDougal's Christian name?"

The governess only looked at her with twinkling eyes. Father chuckled.

"You ken better than that, lassie," he said. "The child's name must no be spoken aloud until the day o' her christening. Would you bring her bad luck by guessing?"

Martha snapped her mouth closed. She did

not want to bring bad luck to her niece. She did not see why saying a baby's name before the christening should bring bad luck, but everyone said it would.

Miss Crow smiled at her.

"There's no bad luck in thinking your own private thoughts, you know," she said.

Martha grinned back. She passed the next two miles in considering the various possibilities for names. She had never thought about naming a baby before, but it now struck her as a most interesting occupation. There were so many names she liked that she soon began to feel one tiny niece was not enough baby to choose for. She decided she would have a great many children herself in order to use all the names she liked best. If Grisie did not use Margaret, then Martha certainly must, for Mum. And Miss Crow's name, Lydia, was like something out of Shakespeare. His plays were full of fine names. Cordelia was extremely nice. Juliet was beautiful, but Martha did not think she would like to name a daughter after a girl who died so young. That made her think of Dead Cora. She was a real person, and somehow it did not seem at all gruesome or unlucky to think of naming a baby after her. Grisie's baby could be another Cora MacDougal—just as bonny and merry as the first one, and (it was to be hoped) far more fortunate in regard to fish.

Cora MacDougal. It was a fine name.

But then, Martha could not help thinking, so was Martha MacDougal.

Slowly, the carriage wound its way north. After a long time, it crested a hill, and Father leaned forward to point out the window.

"Look," he said to Martha. "D'ye see that bit o' blue, there?"

Martha nodded.

"It glitters," she murmured.

"Aye. That's Loch Caraid. And that knob there beside it is the Creag. Nearly all the land ye can see out this side o' the carriage, Martha, is ours. That's where your grandfathers and mine have lived and died, time out o' mind."

Martha stared wonderingly at the quiet hills rolling down toward the wedge of blue loch. She could not see the Stone House, nor any houses at all. They were hidden by the folds of the hills. A stranger who stood atop this hill looking east would have no idea how many lives were being lived in the valley below him, how many fires burning and hearts beating.

"What's out this side, Father?" she asked, turning toward the other window.

"Och, why—mountains, as ye can see for yourself, and west o' the mountains, Loch Lomond," said Father. "And west o' that, the coast and the islands. And west o' that, the sea."

Miss Crow nodded, looking westward with thoughtful eyes.

"Aye, and west of that—America."

"America," echoed Martha. Miss Crow's brother lived there; he was a trapper in the wild northern woods.

"And just below, Balliecruin," said Father. "Look, ye can see the house from here."

Martha craned her neck down and saw the

peaks and turrets of a very large roof. She thought she would burst with impatience during the last long minutes, as the carriage toiled its way down from the hill toward the wide grounds of Balliecruin spread out below.

"I wish I might get out and run," she said. "'Twould be a great deal faster."

"Hush, lass, we'll soon be there now."

And at last they were. Martha had long wanted to see Grisie's grand house, but now she was so eager to get to the baby that she scarcely noticed anything about it except that it was almost impossibly large. The carved oaken doors seemed made for giants. A black-coated butler led them down a long, shining hall with very high ceilings and gold-framed portraits lining the walls. Behind another door was a bright parlor where Mum was waiting to meet them. She held a bundle of soft blanket cradled in her arms.

"Hello," she said, her warm smile shining out. "Softly, now. She's just gone to sleep."

Father held Martha's hand as they went

quietly toward the baby. Mum lowered her arms for Martha to see.

Father was making an odd noise in his throat. He opened his mouth as if to say something, but he did not speak.

"I expect you'd like to hold your niece, Martha?" asked Mum.

"Och, aye!" murmured Martha. No one had to tell her to keep her voice soft. She held out her arms and felt the baby's gentle weight. All she could see among the draping folds of the blanket was a round red face with tiny dark lashes and a small solemn mouth.

"Hello," she breathed. "You dear wee thing. I'm your auntie. I'm your Aunt Martha."

Father went to Mum and kissed her, and they stood together talking in hushed voices. Martha bent her head down close to the baby and kissed a wee red ear.

"I dinna think you look like a Martha after all," she murmured.

The baby gave a little sigh and turned her head into the crook of Martha's arm. Her pink skin showed through the dark wisps of hair on her tiny head. She reminded Martha of Mr. MacDougal, the way he had looked in his bed without his wig. The old lump rose in her throat once more, for it struck her that Mr. MacDougal was this baby's other grandfather just as Dead Cora was her other aunt.

"I hope they *do* name you after her," she whispered to the baby. "And dinna you worry. I'll be twice as good an auntie, I promise. And Father's as good as any two grandfathers. And you've got such a nice father and mother, and three uncles, and the kindest, sweetest grandmother in the whole world. I mean my mum. I dinna ken about your other grandmother, but I expect you'll like her quite well. And when ye're a bit older, I'll make you a fairy doll all your own."

The baby stirred a little, and the delicate eyelids slowly blinked open. Eyes as blue as Loch Caraid stared up at Martha, studying her face. She was such a tiny wee thing, this bairn, as light in Martha's arms as a loaf of bread. She was scarcely anything at all—but she was everything. Martha held her breath, trying with all her might to read the secrets she knew lay hidden behind those searching eyes.

Come Home to Little House

The MARTHA *Years*

LITTLE HOUSE IN THE HIGHLANDS

THE FAR SIDE OF THE LOCH

DOWN TO THE BONNY GLEN

The CHARLOTTE *Years*

LITTLE HOUSE BY BOSTON BAY

ON TIDE MILL LANE

THE ROAD FROM ROXBURY

The CAROLINE *Years*

LITTLE HOUSE IN BROOKFIELD

LITTLE TOWN AT THE CROSSROADS

LITTLE CLEARING IN THE WOODS

ON TOP OF CONCORD HILL

ACROSS THE ROLLING RIVER

The LAURA *Years*

LITTLE HOUSE IN THE BIG WOODS

LITTLE HOUSE ON THE PRAIRIE

FARMER BOY

ON THE BANKS OF PLUM CREEK

OLD TOWN IN THE GREEN GROVES

BY THE SHORES OF SILVER LAKE

THE LONG WINTER

LITTLE TOWN ON THE PRAIRIE

THESE HAPPY GOLDEN YEARS

THE FIRST FOUR YEARS

The ROSE *Years*

Little House on Rocky Ridge

Little Farm in the Ozarks

In the Land of the Big Red Apple

On the Other Side of the Hill

Little Town in the Ozarks

New Dawn on Rocky Ridge

On the Banks of the Bayou

Bachelor Girl